MisGuided
JUSTICE

An Offending Defensive Play

by ROGER WRIGHT

Misguided Justice
- An Offending Defensive Play
Copyright © by Roger Wright, 2018

FIRST EDITION

ISBN: 978-1-7324638-0-6

This book may be ordered on:
www.Amazon.com

Library of Congress in Publication Data

Category: Mystery, Thriller & Suspense

Written by: Roger Wright | bluiewhite59@gmail.com

Cover & Text Layout by: Eli Blyden |
www.CrunchTimeGraphics.com

Printed in the United States of America

Disclaimer

This is a work of fiction. Names, characters, businesses, places, events, locales, and incidents are either the products of the author's imagination or used in a fictitious manner. Any resemblance to actual persons, living or dead, or actual events is strictly coincidental.

Dedication

To Deanne Albala, my muse.
She's been a real help to me in so many ways.

Table of Contents

MisGuided JUSTICE

An Offending Defensive Play

CHAPTER ONE

It is the third of October, 1995 at the Superior Court in Los Angeles, California, where the foreman of the jury has just entered the room. He is a middle aged Hispanic man, who appears weary from the seven hour and fifteen minute sequestered jury deliberation. He ceremoniously hands the verdict to the Bailiff who presents it to the judge who is sitting high up on the bench in his black robe. Judge Mutsuhito Ota, a fifty five year old Japanese American, is well respected for his impeccable record of fairness and calm temperament. This has been a difficult trial with enormous media attention. Emotions have been high for weeks now awaiting a final verdict.

A hush falls over the crowded courtroom where a person could hear a pin drop, the tension is enormous awaiting resolution on this showcase trial. It is a pivotal moment in what has been called the trial of the century. A noted athlete, a local and national hero, an All-American football player at UCLA, former Heisman Trophy winner and Most Valuable Player in the Rose Bowl. He is a native son, having been born in Oakland, California and was the NFL number one draft pick when he graduated with a degree in Black Studies. He had played ten years for the Los Angeles Rams, winning them their first and only Super Bowl. Designated M.V.P. for that game, he had been an All Pro for nine of the ten years he played for the Rams. He was also the first running back to rush for over three hundred yards in one game and held the record for most rushing yards in one season at 2,476 yards. The first N.F.L. player to be given a million dollar a year contract, he made more millions with his many product endorsements and personal appearances. At the end of his illustrious career, he played three more years on wobbly knees for the Oakland Raiders. As Oakland was his hometown, every political party wanted him to run for office. He respectfully declined.

A light skinned Afro-American, well loved by both black and white sports fans, he was in the same league with the legendary Mohammed Ali for the greatest American athlete of the century. Like Ali, he earned an Olympic Gold Medal. He had amazing speed, and as a sprinter was part of a world record four hundred meter sprint relay team. At six feet four inches with a thirty four inch waist and a fifty two inch chest, he weighed in at two hundred and thirty pounds. He was understandably just as popular with women as well as male N.F.L. aficionados. Often married and divorced, he was still very handsome and debonair. He made fresh millions from television advertising, which usually featured his athletic ability; jumping over turnstiles or racing through the airport to catch a plane. Popular with the media—he did live cover for pro-football games. In the off season he worked as a character actor in several feature length movies.

Slowly and with great deliberation Judge Ota reads the verdict the bailiff had handed him. He carefully folds the paper as if it were an origami project, and ceremoniously handed it back to the bailiff. He asked the jury foreman to read the verdict aloud. He admonished the people in attendance to remain quiet. He looked up panned the court room and then pronounced Junias "Jet" Jefferson not guilty of all charges. J.J., as he is known, leapt straight up in his chair, ecstatic in jubilation. Every member of his substantial legal team loses their usual courtroom decorum and commence hugging him and shouting terms of congratulation. It seems that every Black person in the gallery went berserk complete with whooping and hollering. Judge Ota bangs his gavel and calls for order, all to no avail. He gives up in dismay and retreats to his chambers. It has been a long and contentious trial for him with enormous pressure due to close scrutiny by the media. There have been accusations of jury tampering and outrageous bloviating by every single talking head on T.V. and radio. Just getting the trial moved from Santa Monica, where the crime had been committed, to L.A. was questioned as a political maneuver, not just a practicality to access a better venue with a larger jury pool. Now that the verdict had been read the Caucasian members of the gallery sat in stunned, whispering to each other with heavily frowned faces in shocked disbelief.

A similar scene was unfolding at the main branch of Orange County Community College in the spacious second floor cafeteria of the student union building. All ten, 36 inch T.V.s were tuned to the same channel and every single seat was taken. It was standing room only in every doorway, and students, male and female alike had their eyes glued on those T.V. screens. Ricky Lawrence sat with a group of his posse—guys and gals, on a large leather sectional waiting for Judge Ota to hand down the verdict. When it was read, a like reaction to that of the courtroom ensued. All of the Afro-American, and many of the Latino students jumped up high fiving each other, guffawing and celebrating exuberantly in their teenage fashion. Justice had been done as far as they were concerned. The Caucasian crowd, the Asians, and some Hispanics sat there stunned and perplexed. One by one the speculations of what really happened, and what went wrong with the trial were voiced. Platitudes for the prosecution were heard. Nobody could understand why J.J. had not been found guilty. Ricky and two of his friends left after a while and had a twenty minute discussion about it in the parking lot before they split up and went their separate ways home.

Back at the Lawrence residence, a similar discussion was underway.

"Can you believe that lousy verdict Bob, not guilty, my ass, he was as guilty as sin and you know it", said Bob's wife Jean. She was pissed off at a very high level, and Bob knew when to be quiet and let her vent.

"I watched the whole damned trial on T.V. at work from beginning to end for the last six months, that son-of-a-bitch, J.J. killed his wife and her boyfriend, just as sure as God made little green apples. It was plain and simple, cut and dried, a dunce could have convicted him."

Bob, a gold shield detective on the Los Angeles Police Force sat impassively, and continued to listen as Jean, an accountant at a local Ford dealership ranted on. She was on a roll and he, a cop, was privy to insider information, and had a perspective all his own. He would listen and wait his turn to speak. He had watched bits and pieces of the trial, and was saddened at the outcome. In a way it had broken his spirit, because he had been a big fan of J.J.'s over the years. Every red blooded Los Angeles male football fan—black, white, yellow, red or tan loved what J.J. had done for the lowly Rams.

"Never would have won that super bowl without him", was frequently heard when J.J.'s name came up in conversation. And, it wasn't just in L.A. that his alleged misdeeds were sensationalized; the media dubbed it the "trial of the century", and his legal defenders "the dream team". It seemed like every pro football fan in America was rooting for him.

Poor Bob, hoping to derail Jean form her vitriolic furor pitched in, "Thinking about dinner, Honey, I have to work tonight?"

"Not right now Bob, let's wait until Ricky gets home and see what he wants to eat." She doesn't want to cook tonight he surmised. It's either going to be Chinese carryout or pizza and wings. Either way, I'm good, he thought.

"You know Bob," it was starting again. "Right from the get go that bogus alibi of his with the cut hand on a glass he supposedly broke at the conference in Chicago the very next day: it was a lie." Jean shakes her head of red hair and snarls, "And the butcher knife he bought just two weeks before the murders is missing and he can't remember where it is or how he lost it. What a crock of shit that was." She stares at Bob wanting confirmation. He just sits impassively and shrugs his shoulders. "Another bold faced lie, you just don't lose or misplace a friggin' butcher knife."

"We know where the knife is Mom", Rickey interjected as he entered through the kitchen screen door of their Hollywood Ranch style home.

"Shut up Ricky," she wasn't finished, "and then he attempts to flee in the white GMC with his buddy."

"It was a white Mercury Mountaineer, Mom.

"Okay, a white Mountaineer, the bastard was heading to the airport with that other NFL loser, Leontis something or other. Someone spotted them and called the police."

"His name is Leontis James, Mom, he played defense for the Oakland Raiders for a dozen years a real hitter", Ricky piping in again.

"Anyway, she continued, "That dumb thirty-five mile per hour chase, with twenty cop cars in pursuit and helicopters zooming around like hummingbirds—Jesus what a farce." She rambled on, "So when he gives up, what's J.J. got in the car that Leontis is driving, a .357 Magnum, a passport, eight grand in cash, a disguise, a packed bag, and a plane ticket to Bora Bora. Now I ask you Bob, does that look like an innocent man to you?"

Bob was getting hungrier and impatient, but now his son Ricky was in gear.

"Yeah Mom, the disguise was a good one, ha ha, dark glasses a fake beard, a moustache and a faggoty Tam-o-shanter hat. Like nobody at the airport was going to spot him in that get up." Ricky loved it when his mother got all riled up about things, but was always able to loosen her up with his teenage opinions. She was laughing now too as was Bob.

"It's still a travesty of justice don't you agree?" directing her question back to Bob. Bob just acted bewildered and turned his palms up on the captain's chair he was sitting in. It was his no comment answer.

"Can we think about dinner, Dear?"

"In a minute Bob," now directing her venom to Ricky. "The preponderance of evidence the forensic guys came up with from J.J.'s pad unbelievable: bloody socks, bloody gloves, a bloody shoe, his size. A footprint found at the scene of the crime was determined to be the same size and same distinctive brand, Giorgio Britani's. How could the prosecutors miss?" She shook her head again in disbelief. "Add to that hairs from the navy knit hat found at the scene matching J.J.'s DNA, he might just as well left his wallet there too."

Taking his mother's side, Ricky pitched in, "Dad, we studied all that stuff in my forensics class. We did it two ways. First the L.A.P.D. forensics guys used polymerase chain reaction, and then restriction fragment length polymorphism just to be sure about those hairs."

"That's a real mouthful Rick," said his dad, "biggest words you ever used in your life son."

"I go to college, Dad" he said snidely. Bob had only attended the Police Academy which was run at a non-college venue, and granted no degree. At the end of his patience, Bob felt it was time to add his two cents.

"Hold it everyone," raising his hands in 'praise the Lord' fashion, "I'm not saying J.J. was or wasn't guilty, but I just have to point out a few things to you two. First, there were no eye witnesses to the crime, second, there was no confession by the accused, and third, and most importantly no murder weapon was found. All the other stuff is circumstantial evidence and even the flight in Leontis Mountaineer could be justified in that J.J. was scared. It's the way the courts and lawyers look at things."

"Yes Bob, but J.J. was a jealous man, a wife beater with a restraining order against him. He had motive, opportunity and enough circumstantial evidence against him for Misty Colchester and Bruce Blackwell to convict him ten times over."

Ricky interjected, "and that Leo James, his buddy, the one who drove the Mountaineer, he ain't no angel himself. In my opinion he's got the knife. He's holding it in safe keeping like a 'get out of jail free card', you wait and see."

"Is that what your pals think, Rick?" asked Bob.

"Yeah, it is—Leo James has a record, he's always been a bad boy, reveled in it, it was part of his M.O., as a hit man on the Raiders."

"Say are we going to eat tonight or just re-try J.J. in absentia?" Bob was checking his wrist watch when he asked that question. "I have to work in two hours."

"Okay, okay," Jean said still pissed off, "Let me get something going. Ricky, if you have some homework you'd better get on it. What do you want for dinner, Bob?"

"Wings and pizza, and antipasto salad from Bassano's sounds good to me, Dear."

"Okay, Bob, I'll make the call; what do you want on the pizza?"

"Pepperoni, onions and black olives."

"Delivery or pick-up?"

"Delivery, Honey, I need to shower and shave, I worked out at the gym today and I feel scuzzy."

Ricky had already left for his room and would eat anything that came in the door with his bottle of Mountain Dew to wash it down with. He was in his room now breaking in a new 'game boy' as Jean made the phone call to the pizza shop.

CHAPTER TWO

Later that evening Bob and his partner, Larry Giles, a newly promoted gold shield detective, were sitting in an unmarked car staking out the home of a highly suspected drug dealer. They were shooting the breeze, rehashing the events of the trial especially the verdict that had come out that very same day.

"At least there weren't any riots down in Watts like they predicted if the verdict went the other way, Larry".

"Yeah, and a good thing too, this whole issue got the race card thrown at it by J.J.'s attorney, Johnny Hudson. He was the only Black attorney on the so-called 'Dream Team'. The whole jury was just looking for any excuse to pounce on a not guilty verdict." The jury of twelve, was comprised of nine Black women, two Hispanic men and one Caucasian woman. Larry, a man of color, like J.J., had been born and raised in inner city Los Angeles, and as such, was street-wise. He understood the ways of the 'hood' and the criminal types who frequented it. After serving four years in the US Army as an M.P., as soon as he got out he applied to the police academy. He graduated with no difficulty, became employed immediately and quickly rose through the ranks to become a detective. Some said his promotion was token service to placate L.A.'s black population, because there were so few men of color on the L.A. police force. Those who knew Larry, knew that it was not true. Larry was a darned good cop. Above reproach, and Bob was happy to have him as his partner. Bob's military experience had been in the Air Force where he served as an air traffic controller. Bob had a few years of experience on Larry and was known as a top flight detective himself.

"It just seems so strange to me, Larry with all the circumstantial evidence, plus motive and opportunity, that J.J. had, that Misty Colchester and Brad Blackwell, the prosecutors couldn't get him convicted."

"There was a lot of confusion early in the trial, Bob. Remember all the interviews with folks who heard dogs barking, door slamming and saw shadowy figures walking about the property. It was all a smoke screen. The 'Dream Team' lawyers especially A.J. Davis, the dude who read the letter J.J. supposedly wrote for the media when J.J. didn't show up to turn himself in when he was scheduled to."

"Yeah, I remember him, J.J.'s personal legal front man."

"Well that day J.J. was heading to LAX in the white Mercury Mountaineer with Leo James driving."

"Yeah, I recall that too."

"A.J. did that stalling to buy time for the rest of the defense, and it worked."

"Yeah, and like Ben Shapiro, the big time sports lawyer interviewing J.J.'s houseboy, Hercules Merrifield, tell me the 'Dream Team' didn't get to him. His statements and timeline didn't match what Misty Colchester dug out of him on the stand."

"Plainly, 'Herc the Jerk', never was the sharpest pencil in the box. He was banging his bitch girlfriend when J.J. got back from the murders, and needed to get J.J. into the limo that was waiting at the gate to take him to the airport. Herc opens the gate, lets the limo onto the grounds of J.J.'s estate; J.J. gets in and is whisked off to the airport headed to Chicago. J.J. probably told Herc to get rid of the stuff in the laundry hamper right away, and the jerk didn't do it. He figured that J.J. was going to be gone for a few days and Herc was busy with his girlfriend. Herc Merrifield fucked up, it's plain and simple."

"Right on Lar, good call."

"So, like the next morning, Herc hops into the black BMW J.J. probably drove to Bellaire the night before, to take his lady friend home, and lo and behold, who is waiting for him when he gets back to the estate—the whole LAPD with search warrants. Herc never even went into the big house because he stayed in the guest cottage the night before which is where he always slept. The cops find bloody socks, bloody shoes, bloody gloves, and Herc is standing there with his dick in his hand, totally mystified. All the top rank detectives want a piece of this action and this is where that bastard Vance Hubbard fits into the picture."

"I remember Lar, Vance was the racist detective accused of planting the bloody clothes and gloves in J.J.'s house and just wanted to see J.J. get his ass hung out to dry. Or so it seemed."

"And seven months of trial elapsed before all that came out, thanks to Dutch Van Cortland, another racist who was the chief investigator at the scene of the crime where Danielle lived."

"So you think he's a racist too?"

"Not sure, could be."

"But Lar, Hubbard was there too, we were all aware of that."

"Here's the thing, Bob, with all those cops and detectives swarming all over the scene, it would have been impossible for Vance to scoop up all that evidence unseen, and then plant it later at J.J.'s estate. Think about it; that stuff was already there, no planting needed."

"I agree Lar, it would have been a stretch; I guess we all kind of knew it as did the judge, the jury and the two prosecutors. And get this Lar, it may make sense to ditch your bloody gloves and shoes at the scene of the crime, but nobody takes off their pants when they are running away—nobody."

"That's what I'm saying Bob, the prosecution had him by the balls even without the murder weapon. Up until a few weeks ago when Johnny Hudson put on his magic show with J.J. in court tying on the dried out bloody gloves."

"Yeah, famous lines: 'If the gloves don't fit, you must acquit', what a farce that was."

"So you're saying Hubbard was set up?"

"Exactly, the 'Dream Team' had it all scoped out. First they hear Hubbard the racist never even used the 'N word', then they find out from Colchester and Blackwell that he did, and it was all on tape and in the records."

"I remember now Lar, Ben Shapiro, the New York City guy who got Hubbard up on the stand to make statements of denial and then Blackwell cross exams him and he starts taking the fifth amendment. Blackwell and Colchester tricked the dumb bastard."

"No Bob, it was not trick, he perjured himself alright, but he was prepped and the prosecutors fell into the trap that had been set for them. There is no doubt in my mind Hubbard was sought out and bribed big time by the 'Dream Team'. He castrated himself on the stand, for which he became a multi-millionaire. I'd bet my pension on it."

"They were desperate weren't they Lar, didn't want to lose the trail of the century; all those big egos. Probably chipped in half a million each to get him to say that he never used a racial slur. They knew that the prosecution would sandbag him. You know what was really interesting, that nobody could figure, was why F. Lee Montgomery quit the team early … he knew that they were losing, didn't he?"

"Sure and they got that bitch Tracy Felton to take his place and offset Misty Colchester for the TV audiences. Bought them some more time to lay a plot, get J.J. off and blame the murders on some mysterious intruder that they never caught. That was just more drama; Tracy, the sexy one going head to head in the courtroom with Mistry about all that nickel and dime stuff, that had no real bearing on anything."

"So what we really have Lar, is Hudson, Shapiro, A.J. Davis and Melton pulling this off."

"They are smart Bob, evil, but smart, bought themselves some time."

"And now there's nothing we can do about it. It is now a case of double jeopardy being what it is, unless some compelling new evidence surfaces, which isn't likely."

"The whole thing stinks Bob, it's a miscarriage of justice and that poor guy Anton Sartre, the boyfriend lover of Danielle's, he sure picked a bad night to jump her bones."

"You got that right Bob, wrong place at the wrong time and J.J. stabs him while he's humping her on the couch, blood squirts everywhere, and then the son-of-a-bitch cuts the poor guy's throat. She jumps up and grabs a lamp, knocks the knife out of J.J.'s hand and she grabs it trying to defend herself. She cuts J.J.'s hand through the glove, but he wrestles her to the ground and takes the blades away from her. Him being six foot four and two thirty, he overpowers her, a slender woman, maybe one twenty dripping wet, and he kills her in a fit of rage."

"There was a ton of knife wounds on her body as I recall."

"Yeah, like eleven, and then he slashes her throat just to be sure."

"T.V. tonight said Anton Sartre's family is planning a civil suit so we'll see what happens there."

"Should be interesting Bob, wait and see."

Talked out, Bob said he was going to doze off a bit while Larry kept his eye out on the target property. Another hour passed and at about 2:15 am Larry shook Bob awake.

"Wake up Bob, looks like we have some activity here, black Caddy just pulled up in front of the house, and tossed something out on the lawn."

"Bet it wasn't the newspaper Lar, hit the siren and the lights, and let's see what it is."

CHAPTER THREE

Two weeks passed after the verdict of the 'Trial of the Century'. Bob and Larry had made a good bust on the drug dealer on their stakeout. The talking heads on T.V. and radio jocks had their field days, but were already starting to simmer down looking for the next big story. The people of L.A. were back to reality too; eat sleep, work and whatever, with only an occasional comment about the trial. Jean, Bob's wife was not happy about the verdict, and had taken her son Ricky's opinion of Leontis James, and the missing murder weapon to heart.

At dinner one night, Bob remarked to Jean, "Back to normal now are we Honey?"

"What do you mean normal?" she retorted.

"Well you've been out of sorts ever since that verdict came out you know."

"Are you complaining that you haven't been laid in two weeks Bob, well if you are, alright; I'm still pissed about it, and the lackadaisical attitude you took about it. You know damn well J.J. was a guilty as sin."

"What I know and what I can prove in a court of law are two different things, dear. It's the law, the courts, politics, race relations, jury composition, judge selection, a lot of things—it's not that simple. I'm sorry, but that's the way I see it, the big picture; I'm a cop."

"Well I'm sorry too I guess; I empathize with his poor dead wife, Danielle. I've been bitchy, just eat your pot roast, you'll get your reward later," smiling as she said it. He smiled back at her affectionately.

"Thanks Honey, that's my girl. So where's Ricky tonight?"

"New intramural basketball league started up at school. He and some of his friends got a team together and their first game is tonight."

"Good, he needs the exercise."

"There's something else I wanted to tell you about Bob, promise you won't get mad at me, okay?" He nods for her to continue. "I really want to make love with you tonight sweetheart; women get horny too you know."

"Really" acting surprised, but not really. "Go ahead spit it out, Honey, whatever it is. I'm not going to mess up a good roll in the hay," Bob acting and sounding very playful.

"Well, it got me to thinking about what Ricky said about that knife and how Leontis may have hidden it to use later as evidence to save his own sorry ass from serious jail time."

"So, go on."

"Leontis James leases that Mercury Mountaineer from our agency, you know, the one he drove J.J. around in on the day they caught up with him heading to the airport."

"So?"

"I started looking into his financials. J.J. put up the money for that car and signed on it as co-signer. Leontis would never have gotten it out of our showroom otherwise. We do credit checks on all our customers. I have access to it all because I'm the agency's chief accountant."

"And", Bob is all ears now.

"Leo, as he likes to be called, has basically squandered all his N.F.L. loot and lives on a modest pension."

"He was never a big star like J.J. Honey."

"I get that Bob, he lives in a modest walk-up apartment in Culver City. He and J.J. it seems went to the same high school in Oakland. He has no job, and doesn't have a college degree; just a certificate of attendance. He never even declared a major at San Diego State College, and basically sticks around J.J. Jefferson as his bodyguard."

"Yeah, well, we kind of knew that Honey, but Leo was a real hitter, went in the third round of the draft to the Oakland Raiders."

"Is that so?"

"Yup, he was a real quality player, tough as nails. He never commanded the millions that his pal J.J. did, no commercials, no post season interviews with Larry King, no endorsements. He was a basic ham and egger, a good cornerback, made all pro one or two years, and a solid player for a dozen years for a mostly losing team."

"I'll grant you that he was a really good football player Bob, but his debt ratio is horrible. He's got a record of repossessed cars, a bankruptcy, and foreclosure on his house, late payments on everything. Not to mention overdue alimony, child support payments, debts everywhere and a police record as well."

"How do you know about the police record?"

"We have to Bob, can't have felons and the like renting or leasing our vehicles; you'd be surprised how many try; it's all public record. And that's not all, he's got D.W.I.'s, speeding tickets, drug use, weapons possessions, and female assaults going way back. There is also a sealed juvie record to boot that stinks to high heaven. He's lucky that he's not in prison. I found out with a little digging, he was passing bad checks, pimping and selling stolen goods to pawn brokers as a teenager to buy scat. He's a really bad apple Bob, and a leopard never changes its spots. Past behavior is the best indicator of future behavior you know."

"Who knew," Bob said seeming astounded and shaking his head. "Al Davis owner of the Raiders or somebody in his front office cover-up all that shit—bad publicity for the team."

"Not necessarily for the Raiders Bob," she laughed, "They have a reputation for that stuff anyway."

"But you are right dear, we hold these athletes in such high esteem and blow it off as part of their machismo when they act like bad asses."

"Bottom line Bob, the tale Ricky told us might very well be true. Leo could have stashed J.J.'s knife and told J.J. that he tossed it in the Pacific. There's no doubt in my mind with his putrid record, he'd use that knife as a 'get out of jail free card' if he ever had to save his butt from a long prison sentence."

"I have to admit you've done your research Jean, you make a good case for Ricky's hunch," said Bob scratching his chin.

"Why don't you look into things on your end Bob, and see what you can dig up."

The very next day at Dunkin' Donuts Bob and Larry decided to dig into the evidence of the crime of the century which preceded the trial of the century. It took them several weeks of tedious review of testimony, police records and time lines, as they tried to trace the path of the key piece of missing evidence; the murder weapon. J.J. had bought the knife several weeks before at a high end cutlery store in nearby Brentwood. They interviewed the owner who was also the storekeeper, and he remembered the sale, in vivid detail.

"It was an exquisite meat butchering knife," he said. "Professional quality made of Solingen steel from Germany. It had a mahogany handle and was over twelve inches in length. It was sharp enough to shave with, a real beauty. Mr. Jefferson paid $168 for it plus tax, it was worth a lot more, but he bargained me down."

"Did he say what he was going to use it for?" Asked Bob.

"No Mr. Jefferson just smiled and said something like 'to good use', I don't remember his exact words. He paid in cash and left; the knife came in a special box with a sharpener."

The detectives left. "And the next time it showed up was when J.J. butchered Danielle and Anton, and got blood on his shoes, socks, gloves and pants."

"Yeah Bob, and Herc Merrifield was lying to cover his own butt about never having anything to say about J.J., the night he boogied off in the limo to LAX."

"It didn't really matter what he said or didn't say Lar, in the grand scheme of things. The way I see it there were two soft spots that came into play. First the twenty four hour video footage of

Danielle's house and property that showed a large man with a hoodie seat shirt crossing the lawn from an adjacent yard, and then going right to the front door. J.J. likely still had a key even though there was a restraining order in place to keep him away from her house. He had previously harassed her and stalked her issuing death threats. There is a documented history of him physically abusing her. The culprit is seen on the tapes leaving the house from a side door off the garage. The culprit didn't seem to be discarding anything at that time although the lighting was really poor and there was no moon that night. Secondly, there was never any evidence of breaking and entering and, as Hudson so vividly pointed out, the front door was open."

"Of course J.J. didn't lock it on his way out Bob."

"Naturally, then all that baloney about a dog barking and a small dark car speeding down an adjacent street with its lights off around that time is just bogus."

"Coulda been the black BMW, and the forensic guys never checked it because the only cars in J.J.'s garage were the red Ferrari and the white Bentley, either of which would have been easily recognizable to an onlooker even at night."

"When Herc Merrifield pulled into the driveway the next morning they probably thought that it was his car and never checked it."

"A day later Herc had his car detailed. Isn't that interesting? Do you think that maybe Dutch Van Cortland, Hubbard and Herc the Jerk were in cahoots?"

"Maybe they were both really good detectives once Lar."

"Guess we'll never know Bob."

"So where do you think Leo hid the knife if indeed he did hide it?"

"No place in his apartment or car or anyplace somebody might stumble onto it, maybe figure out what it was and what it could be worth."

"I guess I'd hide it someplace really safe, like a safe deposit box. I'm going to check around Lar, and see if old Leontis James opened up a safe deposit box the day after or thereabouts. That's what I would have done."

Bob did check, and at the fifth bank he came to, the First Union Bank of California, he found that Leo had indeed opened up a box the very next day after the infamous white Mountaineer ride with police and helicopter escort.

Later that week, "We would need more evidence or a stronger suspicion to get a court order to open that box," said Larry.

"And you know Lar, Anton Sartre and Danielle Supon's families have filed a civil suit against J.J. There's going to be all new attorneys, prosecutors, and a new judge at a court in Bellaire. This might not be the best time to muddy the waters with this new knife business."

"I hear you Bob, and there's not going to be an almost all Black jury this time either. It was all over the news this morning. That super douche bag F. Lee Montgomery is back as head of the defense team to ty to redeem himself after quitting on the "Dream Team"."

"He's going to lose again Lar, this time for sure."

"Got a new judge too, another Japanese fellow, Hiroshi Kuroda,"

"Kuroda—well, well, well, I know him, he's a no nonsense guy. There won't be any fucking circus this time, and no T.V. cameras in the courtroom. They have plenty if the right evidence to convict J.J. this time." Larry seemed so pleased, he paid for their lunch at Five Guys Hamburgers.

CHAPTER FOUR

It was Bob's turn for lunch this time, he chose China Garden for chop suey and chow mein. They liked to vary their diet a little.

"Fill me in some Bob, on this civil trial procedure; my experience has been all criminal trial action."

"Well, first off, the burden of proof for conviction is way less. If they, the prosecutors can come up with a preponderance of evidence, just 50% of J.J.'s responsibility for the murders, he's cooked."

"Not beyond a reasonable doubt?"

"Nope not even close, and no unanimous decision either, only nine of the twelve jurors need to agree for a verdict to be reached. The biggie in my mind is that in a civil suit J.J. will have to take the stand, something he was never compelled to do in the criminal case."

"Jesus Bob, it's a sure thing this time, look at the mountain of evidence, the blood, the shoe print, the fibers, videos; a whole lot of stuff never came into play the first time around. I wonder what the damages are going to be."

"It'll be in the millions and there's even more pressure being put on this by all the white folks who were pissed off about the verdict in the criminal trial."

Over the next few months, with close attention from the reporters and T.V. journalists, who drummed up the public interest by exacerbating every point and expanding on every nuance, it became clear that J.J. Jefferson was going to be the loser in this trial. They kept pounding the story turning it into scrambled eggs even though every reader and listener already knew the final outcome. It was just a matter of how much.

During the trial, a video appeared and was shown on T.V. of J.J. wearing the infamous gloves that Danielle had bought him at Bloomingdale's in N.Y.C. with a credit card account she had back there. The records showed that only two hundred pairs of those very expensive gloves had been sold in his size, XL. The same was true of the shoes, the very expensive ostrich skin, Giorgio Britini's in size twelve. Only two-hundred ninety pair were sold worldwide. In the video he was wearing those shoes at several NFL games that he had done live cover for. This totally contradicted what the defense had said at the first trial: he had never owned those shoes or gloves. This lie had led into Johnny Hudson's case that those items belonged to a drug dealer that Danielle had been buying cocaine from. Johnny hinted that the unknown drug dealer had a grudge against Danielle for reasons he couldn't explain. He said all the evidence was planted to make J.J. look like the intruder. He wanted to set up the scene of 'if the glove don't fit, you must acquit.'

One of Danielle's blond hairs was found on the gloves, and fibers from J.J.'s hooded sweatshirt were found on Anton's body. These and blood matches on the gloves, socks, shoes and J.J.'s own blood on his own driveway were all the jury really needed for a negative verdict against J.J.. The prosecutors were very thorough leaving no stones unturned. Reports of D.N.A.

testing started floating in from eleven independent agencies paid for by anonymous donors. They added more fuel to the fire of guilt. D.N.A. testing is very time consuming, taking months, in some cases years. The findings were most enlightening.

J.J.'s blood matched .05 percent of the base population or about one in 170 million, making it unlikely that the samples came from some random intruder. Danielle's blood found on his socks and gloves had a one in 21 billion chance of another match. Likewise Anton's blood on J.J.'s socks and shoes, had a chance of one in 41 billion of another match. Additional police reports of J.J. stalking Danielle, and threatening to kill her from witnesses never called at the first trial, to give testimony, overwhelmed the no nonsense judge and jury. F. Lee Montgomery, J.J.'s star attorney was slapped down every time he protested, and he finally gave up. The last but not least bit of damming evidence was an admission of guilt vicariously by J.J. himself. During his initial incarceration he had been visited by a jailhouse minister and former N.F.L. great, one Roosevelt Steer. J.J. had told Rosie Steer that he did it, and that confession had been overheard by a jailor, who took the stand and tattled. F. Lee Montgomery did protest that one and it was declared not admissible, but the cat was out of the bag. Another witness came forward and stated that Hudson had given J.J. medication to make his hands swell before the glove "try on" charade.

The jury of nine white women, one black man and two Asian men deliberated exactly four minutes before coming up with a unanimous verdict of guilty. The award of damages was

8.5 million dollars to be equally divided between the Supon and Sartre families, but the real issue had been settled. J.J. had done it, and some justice had been served.

There was an enthusiastic but somewhat subdued celebration by the mostly white courtroom audience, as well as the nation as a whole. There were no riots in the streets or protests of any kind. The extra duty police were called up in anticipation of trouble were never challenged. There was much rancor on the part of the black community of L.A., but no violence. In their eyes J.J. was innocent and always would be. J.J. was financially ruined, forced to sell his estate, several businesses he owned or had interest in, all of his stocks and bonds, his flashy cars and all of his household belongings. He was able to keep his beach house in Malibu and, ironically, his black BMW.

A few days later, Bob and Larry met at Freddy's Donut Shop in Santa Monica as part of a team getting ready to bust a home where suspects were making speed from over the counter drug store products in the garage.

"Your wife happy now Bob?"

"Yeah, still moaning he should have been convicted the first time around, but she's okay now. How about you, Larry?" Bob asked being sensitive to Larry's skin color.

"It was a good verdict Bob. I think the first trial was a sham. Hudson played the race card and he won."

"I concur," stated Bob. "Funny hearing you say that Larry— don't take it personally."

"Funny nothing Bob, I might be as black as midnight, but I'm not stupid, and not a racist. Black folks know that too, most of them anyway, it's just all the years of injustice, all the profiling you know, it's their collective reaction to a highly visible case like J.J.'s that mobilizes their pent up anger."

Silence—sips of coffee, bites of donuts.

"So are we done with this whole thing Lar?"

"No I don't think so, I know it's not our case or anything, but we still have the trial of that scumbag detective, Vance Hubbard, who perjured himself. Something might come of that."

"We'll have to follow that one on the networks, Lar, they moved the trial out of town to Sacramento. Said they had trouble finding a jury that could be unbiased…what a joke that is, it's political and we know it."

"Good old boy system at work. Funny how they waited till the civil trial was over before they made that announcement."

"I'd say we keep our ears close to the ground and keep snooping."

"Why's that Lar?"

"I think he was bribed big time, enough to perjure himself. There's got to be a money trail and I think I know where to start."

"And we still got the knife, at least we think we know here it is. I mentioned our suspicion to the Assistant District Attorney, Earl Leonard, but he said insufficient cause, and he thought they had enough evidence to convict when the criminal trial was rolling. Anyway it is a moot point now.

"Well not that moot Bob, if Leo pulls the dagger out, the door opens up all over again…fresh evidence."

CHAPTER FIVE

Having moved Detective Vance Hubbard's trial out of town to Sacramento and delayed it several months past the civil trial of J.J. Jefferson, the public's interest in the whole Danielle S. Jefferson, Anton Sartre murders and its offshoots had waned. Conversely, so had media attention. Vance Hubbard was on trial for perjury. He denied that he was a racist even though all the evidence against him was on tape and could not be denied. The prosecutors were hand-picked by the Attorney General under the sharp eye of Governor Arnold Schwarzenegger. The prosecutors were sternly warned not to confuse the issue at hand with any questions about the planting of the evidence from the Jefferson-Sartre murder trial. It turned out, not to matter, as Hubbard pleaded "No Contest" to the charge of perjury. He had already retired from the L.A.P.D. and was collecting his pension prior to taking the stand in the murder trial. He was sentenced to three years of probation and a $200.00 fine or three months in prison. Surprisingly, at his attorney's prompting, he took the three months in prison all of which would be served in the minimum security prison in Sausalito. Known to all as a country club, it was the temporary home to embezzlers, naughty realtors, and tax frauds. He had been advised by his lawyer to sell his home, change his name and eventually move to another state. All this was to assure his personal safety, as Anton Sartre's family was rumored to still be seeking revenge on him. Now they had the money to buy the means to execute a plan, if the alleged threats weren't just all bluster.

"Tell me that wasn't all a political job Bob."

"It was, it certainly was."

Neither Bob nor Larry were disturbed by the verdict, but both were appalled and disgusted by the sentencing.

"He should have gotten a minimum of four years and not at the country club."

"What's done is done Larry, we need to move on. So you think Vance was bribed and the "Dream Team" set up Colchester and Blackwell?"

"Yeah, and it worked Bob, Misty Colchester was so upset by the antics of that bitch Tracy Melton, that she couldn't think straight, and wanted straight answers. She got'em and they were exactly what Hudson and Shapiro wanted her to ask, all that denial of racist remarks; it was all a plan, a trap."

"And Hubbard denies planting the evidence at J.J.'s house. Well, that was of course, the truth, it was there all the time."

"When it came out that Hubbard was a racist, and evidence and testimony proved it, that was all the mostly black female jury had to hear. Hudson's pantomime with J.J. that 'glove don't fit you must acquit' was the nail in the coffin for the prosecution's case."

"Icing on the cake of injustice, Lar."

"You bet, Colchester and Blackwell were outsmarted, it's that simple."

"So if Hubbard was bribed to perjure himself, and take the fall, where's the money."

"Good question and he's laughing up his sleeve about his chicken shit three month jail term and horseshit probation."

"He's retired, he's rich and he's practically in witness protection the way his attorneys have things mapped out for him. But what about the money Lar, how much do you think it was, and where is it now?"

"Think about it Bob, it can't be in his name anywhere."

"Well how about some of his goomba buddies on the force?"

"No way, he had no friends on the force in my understanding and if he did, could any of them be trusted—a shit heel like him has no real friends. I heard he was hated for a ton of reasons, mostly for grabbing all the sweet extra duty gigs for himself because of his rank and seniority."

"Agreed, Lar."

"The way I figure it, is that it's with his family somehow in a secret account in Switzerland or someplace by now. He never saw it or touched it, it was all pre-arranged somehow."

"So, are we at a dead-end Lar?"

"I can't let it go, and neither can you, it's like we're addicted—we need to follow this and maybe, just maybe something will break, and justice will prevail."

Silence and moments of contemplation followed with sips of coffee and bites of crullers. "You know Bob, I've been into this genealogy stuff ever since Hailey's book and movie "Roots" came out in the '70's. I found out that my ancestors were from present day Ghana. They were brought over in the 1700's, and sold into slavery in Charleston, South Carolina. They worked on plantations raising rice, indigo and later picked cotton in Georgia. Life was hard and it's a long interesting story for me. Here's the thing, I anticipated the outcome of the trial, and contacted the Mormon Church up in Salt Lake City, they are whizzes at this stuff. I've been working on Hubbard's family tree for a whole month, I've got his pedigree. He's got local folks and blood relatives everywhere: New Jersey, Ohio, Iowa but none of them close. I've got a good idea where it might have gone."

"Where do you think it is Lar?"

"He's got this first cousin, a little older up in Banff Springs in British Columbia."

"You mean Canada?"

"Yep, married, no kids—own a little motel near the slopes called Juniper Groves."

"Interesting Lar, so you think…"

"Yeah I think…" eye to eye contact, "Oh no, you want me to play Inspector Clouseau, and go up there and snoop around, and see if I can pick up a money trail."

"Good guess Bob," Larry now smiling like a wily old fox. "You told me once that you know how to ski."

"Right," shaking his head. "It's been ten years since I last skied, and my ski are at my brother's place up at Lake Tahoe."

"We need to pursue this Bob, you and I know J.J. is guilty, and so is Hubbard. We're hooked on this and it's a good hunch; I can feel it in my bones."

"If you feel so strongly about it Lar…"

"No, no Bob, first off I don't ski and secondly, I'd stick out like a raisin in an angel food cake up there. You're at bat on this one Bob, I did the research, and you do the footwork."

"Let me think about it Lar, maybe I can get Jean to go with me; we haven't had an adult get away in years."

CHAPTER SIX

Bob did have some vacation time he needed to use up, and Jean had some coming as well. He convinced Jean to come with him as part of an unofficial investigation team, and a private get away just for the two of them. Ricky was old enough now to be left alone, with Jean's brother looking in on him, to make sure that the house was still standing when they got back. They drove up to Lake Tahoe and got their ski equipment, then flew to Calgary in Alberta from Reno, rented a car and drove west into British Columbia, and Banff Springs. Bob had made reservations for a week at the Juniper Grove Motel and Lodge, a medium priced, family owned establishment. It was close to Norquay, one of the ski resorts in Banff National Park.

"Remember Jean, we're not just here to ski, so keep your eyes open, and your ears tuned to anything that would connect the owners to Vance or the money we suspect they might be in charge of." The lodge itself was tucked into a hillside, no Juniper trees in sight, just white and Scotch pines, and a few spruce trees. It looked like a Swiss postcard complete with second story flower boxes, built out of Lincoln logs, featuring a massive stone chimney and cedar shake roofing. The rooms were actually all separate cabins with their own bathrooms and heating units. The bathrooms had been added on at great expense sometime in the 1960's. Prior to that they had been primitive cabins, with the only bathroom in the main lodge, very old world European. It was a cozy looking place, well kept, yet nothing fancy. The main lodge featured a sauna and a hot tub, but that was the only extra amenity aside from the great room and the breakfast room. No lunch or evening meals were served.

When the Lawrence's checked in, Morton and Jenny Hubbard were there to meet and greet them. Both of the Hubbard's were in their early sixties, dressed in heavy flannel shirts, corduroy pants, après ski boots, and down vests. Both wore glasses, had grey hair and looked healthy and happy. They could have been Ma and Pa Kettle. After Bob and Jean checked in, they were shown to their cabin, shown where to park, where to keep their skis and how to adjust the heater in their cute little cabin. Jenny told them about breakfast, and Mort launched into directions to the slopes they were most likely to visit. Jenny interrupted when Mort seemed to be done; "You really must get over to Lake Louise while you're here and take the gondola to the top of the mountain. Bring your camera, it's one of the most famous 'Kodak moments' in North America, the view of the lake is spectacular."

"Another day," chimed in Mort. "Ski the Sunshine Valley Resort, it's my favorite out that way."

"Oh we sure will," said Jean, full of vim, vigor and pleasantry. Bob remained quiet, observing and listening.

"And here is a list of restaurants," said Mort, handing it to Bob. "Our favorite in downtown Banff, is a little German place called the Gasthaus Inn, best Weiner schnitzel you'll ever get to eat." Mort and Jenny were just bubbling over with enthusiasm and information, eager for them to get started at exploring the area.

"We heard about a big hotel here Mr. Hubbard, is that a good place to eat?" asked Bob.

"Yes, Banff Springs Hotel, but a bit pricey; just be sure to go there and see it while you are here. You can rent cross country skis there and ski around the famous golf course at the base of Rundle Mountain. Your legs may need a break after beating the hills with Alpine skiing; Nordic is a nice alternative."

"We will give it a try Mr. Hubbard, you and Jenny have been very helpful."

"Just call me Mort, Mr. Lawrence, we're Mort and Jenny, the Hubbard's."

"Oh just call us Jean and Bob, always have been," giving Jean a playful hug, and Mort a big plastic smile.

"Well, anything you need, just ask us for it and enjoy yourselves, we'll leave you two on your own now."

Back in their cabin Jean started: "They really seem quite chipper for a struggling motel out here in the hinterland. There must be hundreds of fancier, newer places we passed on the road coming in. They all advertised pools, hot tubs, skating rinks, work-out rooms, restaurants with bars and free shuttles to the slopes."

"Maybe it's the price Jean, I don't know, I didn't shop it, but this place isn't cheap either."

"It must be a struggle for these folks to make it, as the maintenance on these old cabins must cost a pretty penny."

"Good point dear, say did you see the new Land Rover parked out front? It had a Juniper Grove logo stenciled on it with the name of the lodge on the doors."

"Wow Bob, those are really expensive runabouts for a place like this, twice as much as a Ford Bronco or Dodge Dakota. The stenciling itself was probably close to a grand."

"Let's just ski for a day or two and let them get comfortable with us Jean; don't let on that I'm a police officer, okay?"

"So what are you Bob?"

"I'm an accountant, a bean counter, nobody wants to hear about the accounting business, it's enough to put any sane man to sleep."

"I'll just say that we work together for the same car agency. I can cover you is they ask any dangerous questions." Bob was suspicious that if the Hubbard's were the one's getting Vance's payoff, they would be cagey about people asking questions, especially about finances.

Jean and Bob skied for three days, and made conversation with the other guests. In the evening, the Hubbard's stayed aloof, letting the guests relax and socialize in the Great Room by the giant fireplace. There was no monster T.V. in the Great Room, which fostered conversation, although each cabin had a new T.V. with cable hook-up.

Conversations in the morning were collective affairs, with other guests, while Mort and Jenny serviced the breakfast buffet, and contributed to a degree. They talked about generic topics like the weather, ski conditions, road conditions, restaurants, local history and the price of gas. The food was really pretty good for a buffet. Mort and Jenny had sweet pat answers at the ready for everything, and made themselves scarce when Bob or Jean attempted to get chummy.

"They are definitely hiding something Jean; they shy away and avoid eye contact if you get the least bit personal. It's not normal for people their age, or people in this kind of business. I've interviewed thousands of people and I can always tell if someone is lying or hiding something."

"These two are going to be a tough nut to crack Bob; let me give it another try with her tomorrow."

The next day at breakfast, Jean made it know she was beat from all the tough trails. She had a sore knee and needed to take a day off and loaf.

"It's what vacations are for Jean, pamper yourself a little" Bob left for Norquay, a tough layout with lots of black diamond runs. Jean plopped into the big couch in the Great Room with her book in the Main Lodge. The Hubbard's two blue eyed Alaskan Husky puppies, about five months old, snuggled with her. Mort stoked the fireplace, then disappeared. Around noon time, Jenny came prancing in having finished her kitchen duties, and began to straighten out the board games and the magazines. She asked Jean how her knee was feeling and then, surprisingly, asked if she would like to have lunch with her.

"Your husband won't be home a minute before 4:30 dear, that's when the lifts close. We can have lunch in my cottage, it's just a few steps from the lodge. You're okay with just that sweater on Jean. It's just a short walk from the lodge; it's warm out today, up to 25 degrees Fahrenheit. We get a lot of

Americans up here, they don't understand Celsius. We have relatives in the states, California, I think."

"Interesting Jenny, I don't remember much about Celsius from my chemistry classes, seems like a thousand years ago." That was not what Jean found interesting, but didn't let on. The Hubbard's cottage was more spacious than the rental cabins and had its own kitchen. Made of round field stones, it had a new roof of architectural singles, and had serpentine electrical wires running along the roof edges to defeat any ice pack build-up.

"Nice roof on your cottage Jen, perfect match for the stone walls, it's just so pretty."

"Yes, our old roof leaked a whole lot, it was the original, and Mister got tired of patching it. Had this one put on last October just before the snow started to fly."

Inside, Jean could see all new Ethan Allen furniture and accessories, as well as new wall to wall Berber carpeting. "Nice place you have here Jen."

"Glad you like it Jean, we recently updated. I always wanted Ethan Allen. Do you want ham, turkey or a tuna melt honey? I can whip up some soup from a tin as well, tomato or chicken noodle."

"Oh, the tuna melt and tomato soup would be divine if it's not too much trouble." Jenny disappeared into the kitchen, but kept on talking. A few minutes later she returned with a tray of food.

"I like to have a lady guest in here from time to time. It breaks up the monotony of my routine."

Guess I'm special, thought Jean. Could it be that you enjoy showing off your new furniture and carpet, now would it? They chatted some more and then Jean picked up a handsome turtle shell souvenir from the coffee table and remarked about it. "It's pretty isn't it; we got that in the Cayman Islands just this past September. It was the first time Mort and I have been away on vacation in twenty-five years. They raise turtles there you know, and you can take a boat ride out and feed the stingrays too."

"Did you?"

"Oh no, but Mort did, I've got the pictures. Let me clear these plates, and I'll get the scrapbook out." She started her clean up. Jean was onto the scent.

"That must have been really expensive to get there from here Jen".

"Yes it was, flew from Calgary to Toronto, changed planes, and then on to the islands. The water there is so beautiful." Jen seemed to swoon, paused then explained: "We came into some money last summer, and Mort said it was time to fix this place up, and have some fun. Mort went right out and bought that Land Rover, four wheel drive, perfect for around here; paid cash for it."

"Really."

"Oh my I'm bragging now."

"Yes you are Jen, but don't stop now", Jean said. Jen quieted thinking that she had said too much.

"It's tough to lose a loved one Jen, old family members, but that's part of life, isn't it?" No reaction. "Bob and I came into some money when his dad passed away; paid for our son's orthodontic work, and a trip to Hawaii for Bob and me. The older folks want us to enjoy what they leave us, it's their final gift to us."

This snapped Jen out of her trance. "Oh no Jean, it wasn't that, Mort's folks left us this place, and that was about it. It was something else, but please don't tell anybody; Mort and some of his pals on the bowling team bought some lottery tickets and one of them won. They split the money evenly among them. We all made out big, it was a blessed windfall. We fixed this place up, and now we will never have to leave."

"I promise Jen, my lips are sealed."

When Bob got home from the slopes Jean related her conversation with Jenny Hubbard to him. Bob commented "There's no way they could afford a new Land Rover, a trip to the Caymans, a new roof, all new Ethan Allen furniture and new T.V.s in all the rooms on the revenue that this place produces."

"And how about those two husky pups Bob, those pups are a grand a piece."

"The story of them winning the lottery seems farfetched. I'm not sure they even sell lottery tickets up here. I'll check at the gas station on the way to town. They'd surely know if one of their own won the lottery. You can't keep luck like that secret very long, especially if it is a bunch of guys who like to drink beer."

"I'll bet you are right about that, Bob."

"And wouldn't you know it, the Cayman Islands. The banks there launder money from crooks all over the world, no questions asked, all in numbered accounts."

"I knew that too Bob. It's just too coincidental isn't it?"

"I don't believe in coincidences Honey, I'm a constant conjunction type guy... detectives are. I'll bet Vance had to give this shrewd old bastard Mort a big chunk of that bribe to even accept the deal to hide his money offshore."

"I think we found out where the bribe money went Bob, but just like the missing knife, what do we do with it?"

"At least we know that Larry's hunch was right. I'll see if I can get some information from the locals. You keep working on Mrs. Hubbard, see if you can wheedle some more information from her. Maybe she will tell you some specifics like what airline, where they stayed, when they went exactly; its evidence we may need at some point."

"Bob, I'll bet she doesn't even know the truth about where the money came from."

"That could be true, she's not the sharpest pencil in the box. Right now he'd be the target, the blood relative."

They both sipped their hot cocoa, wheels turning in their heads. "Right now all we have is persons of interest Jean, Mort Hubbard and Leontis James, that's it." They sipped and pondered, relaxing in their little cabin, the T.V. on, but neither one watching it. Jean broke the silence. "Tell me Bob, exactly why are you and Larry going to all this trouble and where is it going to end? All this sleuthing is not just a hobby for you guys is it?"

Bob answered quickly. "We were both disgusted by the outcome of the criminal trial, and Vance's joke of a trial as well. We are basically seeking justice on both counts if we can get fresh evidence to surface." That answer seemed to satisfy Jean and they climbed into bed.

Bob did check at the gas station and the little General Store before they left town. Yes, they did sell lottery tickets, but no one in Banff had ever won a nickel playing it.

CHAPTER SEVEN

When Bob and Jean got back from Banff Springs, over a year had passed since the end of J.J.'s big trial in L.A. In that short period of time several books had been written and published, including one by J.J. himself. He of course had the serious help of an experienced author and screen writer. J.J.'s book "Let's Say I Did It", sold extremely well at first with a series of book signings in every major city that had a large black population. He and his sidekick, Leontis James were living large off the royalties of that book. Sales were diminishing and the fad, like notoriety of the book had peaked. Soon he would be living on his generous, but not opulent N.F.L. pension, and he still had children to support, and a beach house in Malibu to keep up.

One Sunday, Bob, Jean and Ricky were sitting down after a late brunch and perusing the L.A. Times. Jean was working on the crossword puzzle, Ricky was reading the comics and, Bob the sports section. He was waiting for the Ram's game to begin on T.V.

The Rams had recently moved to St. Louis, but still had their followers in L.A. albeit—not many, thanks to J.J.

"Said in the paper today that J.J. made over half a million on that bogus book of his," Bob stated.

"Something is wrong with our society," retorted Jean, "When a total scumbag like that can make a ton of money with nothing but a pack of lies, after killing two innocent people in cold blood…sheesh."

"And everybody knows it," piped in Ricky; but at least some of that dough will go toward the 8.5 million settlement the families got after the civil trial."

"Yes Rick, but the provisos built into the contract by the publisher's attorney allow him to keep a lot of it, and all of his N.F.L. pension as well."

"And any money he can make in the future from whatever," added Jean.

"I hope the bastard dies poor, but I'm afraid that'll never ever happen."

"You can count on it, Mom, the way he blows through money, you'd think he was still in his prime making big bucks and playing for the Rams."

"How do you know that?" asked Bob, always ready to take Ricky to task on any outlandish statements he made.

"Cause he's a gambler Dad, he and Leo James and some of J.J.'s old posse are off to Vegas partying almost every week-end."

"And you know this how, Rick?"

"Okay, while you were up in Canada with Mom, I took off with some of my friends for a week-end in Vegas for some action ourselves."

"No," said Jean befuddled, "My brother never told me that."

"He didn't know, Mom, he thought we were camping out in the state park up in the Cucamonga Wilderness near Mr. Baldy.

"You lied to my brother!"

"No, Mom, not really; I told him I was going away for the week-end. He saw me take my sleeping bag out to the car and he shouted out: "Mount Baldy?" I didn't say anything so he assumed that's where I was going."

That's a lie of omission Ricky."

"No, it's not Mom…"

Bob interrupted, "Okay, let's not get into that now, I want to know more about what you saw in Las Vegas."

Ricky continued, "We rented a room at a cheap motel, two beds, and we drew straws to see who got them; the other guys and girls get to sleep on the floor in sleeping bags."

"Girls, you had girls with you Ricky?"

"Get real Mom, it's not like we were couples or paired off or anything, it's the nineties, not the fifties."

"Stick to the part about J.J." said Bob.

"Okay, so we're in a casino and we spot J.J. and Leo and his whole pack. They play blackjack at the fifty dollar a hand table, and shoot craps. They aren't winning. Most of his posse are half drunk, hookers laughing their dumb asses off, and hanging on to J.J. and Leo breathing in their ears and tugging at their chains."

"What chains, Ricky?"

"Skip it, dear," said Bob, "go on Rick."

The fellas in the posse are just jock sniffers, you know hangers on, or pimps for the rentals."

"Where did you see them, Rick?"

"Bellagio, Flamingo, Paris, and the last at New York, New York. We went to New York New York to ride the roller coaster and check out the Harley-Davidson exhibition they have there. I made a little conversation with the Harley dude who watches the place, and he said that J.J. and Leo, who we can see at the tables, come here almost every week-end."

"He says to me, they like the MGM, Caesar's Palace, and that pyramid joint, Lexus or Luxor, or something too. The guy says 'you'd never know it, the way those two blow through money.' J.J. got tapped for 8 mill plus in the second trial, that he is feeling the pinch."

"Interesting Rick, very interesting," noted Bob.

"How could you be in those casinos Ricky, you're not twenty-one yet?" asked Jean.

"Yes, Rick, added Bob, "that's a really good question."

"I'm taking the fifth amendment on this one folks."

"Sure Rick, the miracle of modern technology, the Xerox machine," said Bob.

"We're way beyond that Dad."

"So who are you Ricky?" asked Jean.

"I'm still me Mom, just a little bit older. I'll show you the license if you promise not to take it away from me—cost me thirty-five bucks."

"It's still illegal Rick" said Jean.

"I know Mom, but we figure out age the old Chinese way, from the moment of conception, which makes me twenty-one. Think about it Mom, you're all pro-life all the time aren't you?"

"Interesting rationale Rick," said Bob shaking his head.

"Why do we have laws anyway, everyone breaks them" added Jean.

"Tell that to Hudson and the "Dream Team" added Bob.

Later that week, Bob and Larry met and Bob shared the conversation he had with his son and wife the previous Sunday.

"From what I can make of it Bob, J.J.'s funding Leo and soon the windfall they are enjoying from the sale of that dumb book is going to run out. J.J.'s going to be hard pressed to keep up that 'fast lane' lifestyle. J.J. keeps Leo around as his bodyguard and his N.F.L. pension isn't that big. Leo needs J.J., and J.J. needs Leo, a lot of people are still pissed about the acquittal, and would love to rough up Mr. Jefferson."

"Those two are going to need more easy money aren't they Lar?"

"You guessed it."

"So they bear close watching is what I hear you saying Larry."

"That would be my feeling knowing their backgrounds; I just don't know what they might do."

"Wouldn't it be great to catch them at doing something illegal, like robbing a bank, or running drugs?"

"Right, give us a chance to bust them."

"It might even force a showdown between J.J. and Leo; then we would see what shakes out."

"Maybe you and I could run a reconnaissance trip to Vegas some week-end to corroborate Ricky's story and keep tabs on our quarry."

"Let's keep tabs on them locally Lar, and see when they bolt to Vegas next. Then you and I can sneak away ourselves for a look-see."

"Sounds like a good deal Bob" smiling.

"This will be a team effort taking both of us; I'm sure they are wary animals just like those folks up in Alberta."

"Guilty people are like that Lar, they never look you in the eye, and they make shitty poker players, because they can't bluff."

"I'll tell you Bob, I could sure live well on that eighty-five grand a year J.J. gets from the N.F.L."

"Me too, but we aren't them, porking five hundred dollar hookers, and playing fifty dollar hands of blackjack."

"Yeah, even after his career was over, he still had oodles of money from all those endorsements for footballs, jerseys, posters, even junk he had no right to endorse, like kicking tees and such. His name was magic and then all those T.V. commercial adds for car rental agencies, credit card companies, even toothpaste."

"All that dried up with the notoriety and money from T.V. appearances, live color at Rams games, football video games—he was a gold mine."

"And don't forget those cameo roles he played in big screen movies."

"Poor bastard couldn't act to save his ass, but, the money just poured in, remember?"

"He was an idol, thought he was invincible, owned the world, and of course thought that he was above the law."

"And when his trophy wife got sick of his rough handling and divorced him, his big ego couldn't take it and he killed her."

"No moral compass that's for sure, and that poor jerk, Sartre, just got in the way."

"J.J. sure slashed that guy badly, all in a rage that some guy was balling his ex-wife. Forensic guys said he looked like he fell in a paper shredder."

"And now he hasn't backed off on his lifestyle and spending habits; this could be the break we're looking for Bob."

"So what's the next week-end we have off together Larry?"

"I'll check the roster Bob, this will be fun for a change, and I'm not telling the captain about it either; we're under the radar."

CHAPTER EIGHT

"We're in luck Bob, I got us a couple of unsold rooms at Paris, half price on Expedia.com. It's right across the strip from the Bellagio, we can watch the light and dancing water show from the terrace dining area while we eat dinner."

"How do you know about these things, Larry?"

"Everyone know Expedia Bob, they sell off rooms they can't fill just to get you there. They could probably let you stay for free, and make it all aback at the gaming tables, the dining room and the bar."

"I meant Lar, how do you know the Bellagio is right across the strip from the hotel we're staying at?"

"I get out of town once in a while Bob, and not to ski. You're going to love the buffet at the Paris, it's the best."

"Okay hot shot, when do we leave?"

"Friday afternoon, we can drive up in my car and we split the gas and parking, okay?"

"Then why don't we take my car, Lar? I get better gas mileage, easier to park too."

"Forget it Bob, I want to get there fast and your little Mazda doesn't have the powerhouse A/C my F-250 does. We are driving across the Mojave Desert on Route 15 you know and, it's a four hour poke. Two hundred and seventy miles…with the heat in the hundreds."

"Alright, see you tomorrow, let's get a good night's sleep, I got a feeling we won't be sleeping much on this little mission."

"Pack some different outfits Bob, and we can work in shifts to remain as inconspicuous as possible. I'm packing a suit, some casual clothes and some cowboy garb."

"Don't forget the boots Hopalong."

"I can't wear boots and you know it; what are you going to go as?"

"Go as? Well, a clown one night, then a pirate, and finish up as a ballet dancer."

"Then don't forget to take the tights Barbie!"

"I'll figure out something don't worry. This will be a lark for us, not just police work."

They checked in on a Friday night under the big Eiffel Tower at the Hotel Paris, ate dinner on the terrace, and watched the dancing water show across the street at the Bellagio as planned. About 10pm they went out on the prowl. Larry started a Luxor on one end of the strip, and Bob at the other end at the Silver Dollar. Bob found their quarry first, at the Grand Flamingo, where J.J. and Leo had just arrived from a Cirque d' Soleil performance at another hotel. Bob practically bumped into them as they settled in for some gargantuan sandwiches at the casual restaurant of the Grand Flamingo. Bob called Larry on his cellphone. They hooked up and began shadowing the infamous twosome as they traipsed from one casino to the next.

J.J. and Leo picked up a following at Caesar's Palace, and proceeded to move on down the strip with a couple of high priced hookers, and jock sniffers in tow. Larry called them jock sniffers, guys who like to hand around celebrity athletes or entertainers hoping to be noticed. J.J. Jefferson fit that bill. Leo and J.J. would spend an hour at each establishment playing fifty dollar blackjack, shooting craps, and once in a while roulette. They never bothered with the one-armed bandits. Bob would wait outside while Larry tailed, then they would switch positions at the next venue. They always stayed some distance away so as not to be noticed, they sometimes played the slots or even roulette where a few bucks would last a long time.

At New York New York both Bob and Larry watched from the bar as Leo and J.J. ditched the men in the posse, and headed for the elevators with two of the hooker babes. The girls had been hanging all over them rubbing their chests and shoulders, breathing in their ears in a very sensual fashion. No modesty was employed, this was Vegas and, it was all business for these gals. Bob and Larry watched where the elevator went. "Looks like our boys are home for the night up in the Tower Suite."

"One of them anyway Lar, I'm going to take a ride up and see if I can spot which one they are in exactly."

"Hang back good Bob, don't let them get a fix on you, could hurt us later."

"I know, I know."

Five minutes later, Bob was back and they watched as a serving trolley with food and champagne was rolled onto an elevator.

"I'll bet that's going to the party room in the clouds, Bob."

"No doubt about it, let's call it a night, but as least we know where they are staying."

Out of curiosity Larry stopped at the service desk, and inquired about the price on the rooms. The Tower Suite which featured two king sized beds in separate bedrooms with bathrooms also had a four seat hot tub. It rented for a cool one thousand dollars a night, and had an outlandish balcony that overlooked the whole city. J.J. and Leo were living the good life—full speed ahead.

Saturday, Bob and Larry slept in as they assumed Leo and J.J. would after a hard night of feasting, gaming, drinking and sexual frivolity.

"I bet they smoked a few joints up in the tower suite last night Lar."

"And a few lines of coke and some ecstasy thrown in for flavor would be my guess Bob."

The detectives ate a huge brunch at the fabulous Paris buffet and spent some time walking up and down the strip collecting referral cards from the uneducated and unwashed who were handing them out on every street corner. Larry had stared a collection of these cards; each card featured a gorgeous young woman, thinly clad, and recumbent in a very sexual pose. No prices were mentioned just a first name and a phone number. Larry's favorite: Chantel, friendly, interesting and skilled—a pet for any man.

Later Bob and Larry took a workout at the hotel health spa followed by massages, a nap and dinner around 8pm. They started their surveillance at New York New York where Leo and J.J. emerged around 9:30, and hopped onto a free shuttle bus up the strip. Larry got onboard. Bob would follow on the next bus. J.J. and Leo got off at the Venetian Palazzo, an extravagant complex that had its foreground modeled after St. Mark's Square in Venice, Italy. For a price one could take a gondola ride on the two acre reflection pool, and cruise under the Bridge of Sighs replica.

Bob met Larry in the lounge. "Seems like our boys have tickets to the show here tonight Bob."

"Who's on Lar?"

"Cher, but tickets are one hundred bucks a pop, and that's in the ozone."

"They're in there now I guess. Wonder if they had dinner yet."

"Dunno, it's like a stake out now Bob, we just sit and wait until they surface."

Leo and J.J. did stay for dinner and a romp in the casino, then hopped the shuttle back to New York New York, and crossed the street to the Luxor.

"Guess our boys want to stay close to home tonight Bob; why don't you go in and I'll wait at the bar." It was early yet by Vegas standards, only midnight, and J.J. and Leo picked up some immediate friends at the blackjack table. Bob hung back nursing a drink, and playing a 25 cent slot machine. At about a quarter to one, the boys ditched their entourage, and headed back to the entrance. They stopped just in front of a private meeting room with a placard announcing a sports memorabilia auction slated to start at 1 pm., the last show of the night. Held in a private room, it was admission by invitation only, and J.J. and Leo pranced right in. Bob and Leo flipped a coin to see who would go in, Bob won. Larry was free to hold down the bar as

Bob got by the gorilla at the door by flashing his tin without making it too obvious.

Leo and J.J. had seated themselves toward the front conveniently. Bob took a seat in the back now. The show started with the auctioneer, a short heavyset man, with a New York accent, being introduced by one of his support team. The auctioneer's name was Alan Altman, touted to be one of the top purveyors of sports memorabilia in the United States. His coveted collections of football, baseball, basketball and ice hockey keepsakes were considered by sports aficionados to be second to none. Fittingly, it was all top quality, at top shelf prices.

A list of what was to be auctioned had been handed out to everyone in the audience as well as a numbered marker for bidding purposes. Mr. Altman had two assistants, one on the inside of the door, a sergeant at arms type who kept track of who bid, and a runner, who brought up each item from an ante-room behind a paneled screen in back of the dais.

The first item up was a baseball glove used by Mike Schmidt of the Philadelphia Phillies, a hall of famer. Starting bid was fifteen thousand dollars and it went for twenty-five. Each subsequent item presented in turn got a full explanation as to its history and value. The bidding was active, and sales went well. Items were returned to the ante-room, and would be redeemed with a check, cash or credit card following the presentation.

Several pieces of J.J.'s paraphernalia came up for bids, including a helmet and a jersey he wore in his one super bowl win. There was a pair of shoulder pads, cleats, and an MVP trophy from the years he won it, and a bunch of programs he had signed at UCLA. Altogether the loot would fetch at least one hundred thousand dollars. Curiously, Leo and J.J. did not bid on a single item. All the football items went back in the storage area except for one non-eventful Rams game jersey which sold for twenty-five hundred dollars.

It seemed that this was a baseball crowd, hot for the Yankees, Red Sox and Braves memorabilia, not much into football or basketball stuff. One Guy Le fleur hockey stick went for five grand, and a Bobby Orr set of skates for four grand.

Bob noticed Leo and J.J. chatting it up in low tones between themselves anytime one of J.J.'s items came up for bid. Alan Altman wrapped up the whole event about 3am. He was attending to people who had bid to come and retrieve their treasures and pay. Everyone else left and turned in their markers. Then the heavy set gorilla at the door, the other assistant and the runner who presented the items, gathered up what hadn't been sold in boxes and took them upstairs to Altman's suite.

J.J. and Leo retreated to a very private booth out by the bar. Bob hooked up with Larry keeping their targets in sight. Together they nursed their drinks and observed, pretending not to know each other, just chatting two seats apart.

"Bob, I don't like the looks of this, I think these two birds are up to something. Watch their faces, they are way too serious; something's cooking in their little brains."

"Since they have no company, and appear not to want any, I'd have to agree. I bet they don't go back to the gaming tables, and they are drinking soft drinks, hmmm"

"Something is definitely up—let's watch and see what happens."

"You think they might be running low on money, and got jealous when J.J.'s stuff was displayed?"

"I couldn't see their eyes Lar, but I bet they lit up with dollar signs on them. Let's find out at the desk what room or suite Altman is in."

Bob inquired, and yes, Mr. Altman had a suite in the Director's Wing, but they weren't allowed to give out the suite number for security reasons.

CHAPTER NINE

Bob and Larry's police instinct told them that an event was about to happen, and it involved Mr. Alan Altman and his valuable memorabilia. It would involve goods J.J. wanted back, not so much as keepsakes, but to peddle for the big money they could possibly fetch.

J.J. and Leo waited till they saw Mr. Altman's muscular bodyguard come out of the elevator, and moments later they flagged down their waitress, paid their tab and tipped her. Looking about nervously, they headed to the elevators. Bob and Larry had been independently nursing drinks at the bar each staving off the advances of a heavy cruiser looking for a buyer. Late in the evening the professional escorts ended to get aggressive trying to catch a last customer for their services. Bob and Larry took the very next elevator up to the same floor where J.J. and Leo had gone. They both felt that they needed to be there in case something happened. "Let's hover around down the hall like we're looking for our rooms." Bob did the lurking while Larry found an alcove where he was unseen.

J.J. and Leo were at the door to Alan Altman's room knocking to get in. Mr. Altman came and spoke through the closed door; he began brief conversation, and J.J. was admitted. Leo barged in right after him.

Bob and Larry moved quickly and camped on Altman's doorstep. Larry got down on one knee with his ear close up to the door listening. He could hear a conversation, and it became loud and heated. There were sounds of a tussle, and a blow landing, like a punch to the jaw, some furniture tipping over, then muffled voices and silence.

Larry tried the doorknob; it was locked. There was some more chatter between J.J. and Leo and after a New York minute, the door flew open and J.J. came barreling out with a shocked look on his face. He was carrying a pillowcase, which was filled with goods. J.J. didn't stop and bowled over Larry who was still down on one knee listening. J.J. immediately lit out for the stairwell at the end of the hall marked by a red and white sign that said "fire exit only".

Bob reacted in a flash. "I've got J.J. Larry, go see what's up with Leo and Altman." He gave chase to the speedy J.J.

Larry pushed into the room with his Glock in his hand and confronted Leo, who was busy filling a pillow case with sports mementos which were stacked up neatly in the spacious vestibule of the Director's Suite. Leo looked up shocked to see a black man with a hand gun, and he froze. Mr. Altman was on the floor; unconscious and bleeding from a heavy gash on his temple. A half-awake smallish man clad in pajamas stood dazed at the bedroom doorway. A glass coffee table was upside down, the contents of a box of candy strewn about the floor.

"Freeze Leo," ordered Larry. "Drop the bag and get on the floor face down and don't move a muscle or I'll pop you." Simultaneously Larry flipped open his wallet showing Leo his gold badge. "You over there in your pj's get your sorry ass over there and check your boss' pulse."

The man followed instructions "There is none," he said, stammering.

"Then for God's sake, try to stop the bleeding from his head." Perplexed, the man didn't move. "Use your hand or a piece of his shirt, a wash cloth, anything, and be quick about it."

Larry looked for a phone and didn't see one. "What's your name fella?"

"Brad Finch."

"Okay Brad, I'm a cop where's the phone?"

"Over by the sectional end table, it looks kind of like an elephant." Larry kept eye to eye contact with Leo as he flashed his badge to both Brad and Leo. He moved judiciously toward the phone but could see that Leo was eyeing the door. "Don't move Leo, I pull a quick trigger."

"How you know my name, cop?"

"ESP, Leo, ESP."

The desk clerk answered and Larry ordered medical help and a uniformed Las Vegas policeman to come to the suite explaining quickly what had taken place. Within five minutes L.V.P.D. arrived. They got the low down on what had transpired from Larry and Brad. The officers commended Larry for his perception of the evening that had turned ugly, handcuffed Leo and said that they were taking him to the station house on Moreno Street. The E.M.T.s arrived, tried to revive Mr. Altman, and got the particulars from Brad and Larry. Larry told the L.V. cops that his partner, Bob had chased Leo's partner, J.J. Jefferson out the exit and down the stairs. Larry said that he thought J.J. might be headed back to his room at New York New York. They said that they would pursue it.

As it turned out, J.J. was still pretty fast on his feet and had beaten Bob to the ground floor by three flights of stairs. Bobbing and weaving in the crowded streets, J.J. easily eluded Bob, who became winded, and gave up the chase. He headed over to New York New York to stake out J.J.'s room. Within three quarters of an hour, J.J. showed up, and Bob apprehended him in the hallway with his own Glock drawn and gold tin held high. "Put the bag down Mr. Jefferson, you are under arrest."

The bag went down and J.J. retorted, "arrested for what, and who the hell are you anyway?"

"Waving his pistol Bob said: "Get on the ground face down J.J. and be quick about it and I will explain it to you." Bob did and Mirandized him right away. Bob then flagged down a waiter in the hall who saw what had taken place and told him to notify the front desk, and to get a Las Vegas policeman or two up here right away. The waiter was awestruck with surprise when he saw it was J.J. Jefferson on the floor and complied immediately.

Bob was afraid that house security guards might muck up things if they got involved, and was specific with the waiter as to what he wanted. It took a few minutes and J.J. kept mouthing off repeatedly using the word pig. Bob looked at the bag while J.J. ranted on. It was just a bag with two containers of coffee in it from Seattle's Best and some jelly donuts. Where had J.J. ditched the pillow case he wondered?

When the local police arrived Bob explained what had transpired, and J.J. who had simmered down was off to the races again now that he had a new audience. "You cops are making a big mistake here. You got no cause to arrest me and hassle me like this, just cause of a bogus story by this off duty cop from L.A. who don't know shit. Do you guys even know who I am?"

"We certainly do Mr. Jefferson," said Bob. "I was there when you beat it out of Alan Altman's room less than an hour ago. And by the way, where did you stash the loot you stole from him?"

"Don't know about no loot, and I'm getting a lawyer right away and suing you all for false arrest, harassment, and public embarrassment."

"Enough J.J.," as they paraded him through the lobby in cuffs.

"You white cops all alike, just like in L.A., get your rocks off belittling me, an N.F.L. super star and Hall of Famer." He was hustled into a waiting police car at the curb.

As they were getting J.J. into the back seat of the police cruiser, Bob's cell phone vibrated. It was Larry of course. "We're down here with Leo at the Moreno Street Headquarters. What's up with you Bob...J.J. show up yet?"

Bob explained his end of things making sure the two arresting officers, and J.J. heard the conversation. The two Las Vegas cops smiled.

"Moreno Street okay, we'll skip our station house and go straight there, this looks like it's going to be a big one." The other cop smiled; he was a rookie. "And we got the collar Sarge."

"You bet, got lucky, owe it to Officer Lawrence here."

"Only one not lucky here is you J.J.," his hands cuffed behind his back. "You'll have a lot of explaining to do when we get to Moreno Street."

"You'll be real sorry you came up here from L.A." piped in J.J. "I'll be suing you for false arrest Lawrence, and everything else my lawyers can come up with pig."

"You heard him boys, he called me a pig three times now. I'll be the one suing you, not that it is going to matter. We have you on burglary of valuables worth thousands of dollars, flight to avoid arrest, resisting arrest and assaulting an officer of the law."

"I didn't assault nobody pig."

"Oops, another pig, well for your information, the guy you knocked over as you bolted out of Altman's room is an officer of the law."

"Didn't see no uniform or shield."

"No matter J.J., you're the one in big trouble here. If I were you I'd keep my big mouth shut."

It was almost dawn now, 5:30am with pre-dawn light just starting to take the edge off the desert night to the east. Bob was wide awake, exhilarated that he and Larry had caught J.J. and Leo doing something very bad. How bad, time would tell.

At the Police Headquarters Bob and Larry gave their accounts of the evening's activities to the Chief of Police Avery Adams, and two senior detectives, John Watkins and Armando Gutiérrez. Leo and J.J. would each be interrogated individually later in the day. Held in separate cells, they could not communicate with each other. Impressed by the two L.A.P.D.s work, Avery Adams just had to ask: "So what brought you two guys to Vegas in the first place?"

Larry answered with an air of humor in his voice and a smile on his face, "Just a week-end getaway Chief, some light duty gambling, good food, a show or two and a chance to collect as many of those sexy escort cards the wetbacks are handing out on every street corner."

The Chief laughed, he knew better, but didn't want to know the particulars, lest it muddy the waters in court, relative to the arrests. "Good work officers, we'll take it from here. Go back to your hotel and get some sleep, shower, shave, have breakfast, then come back here at 11am. I want you here behind the glass for the interviews with these two birds, and we want to get an interview with Mr. Altman when he wakes up for his end of the story. Oh yeah, and his roomie, what's his name, Brad something or other—we need to interview him too. You guys got Leontis James red handed, but the memorabilia you said J.J. took off with, we need to find that stuff. It'll help build an irrefutable case against J.J. in court."

CHAPTER TEN

Bob and Larry were back at police headquarters at 11am sharp. They were showered, shaved with only three hours of sleep, for the initial interviews of the suspects. They stood behind a one way mirrored glass panel to an interview room with Las Vegas Police Chief Avery Adams and a senior detective, John Watkins. They listened while another senior detective, Armando Gutiérrez entered the tiny room where Leontis James was already seated.

"Leontis James, I'm Detective Gutiérrez here to get your side of the activities last night. Can I call you Leo?"

"Call me whatever you want."

"Would you like coffee or soda?"

"No thanks."

"Okay Leo, what have you got to say?"

"Nothin'."

"Our report says that Detective Giles of the Los Angeles Police Department caught you red handed in Mr. Alan Altman's suite at the Luxor at about 3:30am, is that correct?"

"If you say so."

"The report says you were trying to steal stuff."

"Don't know about that."

"It's part of the report Leo." Leo shrugs his shoulders again, no comment. "It appears Mr. Altman was seriously injured in a scuffle that ensured and no attempt was made to help him."

"Don't know about no scuffle."

"Okay Leo, we know that you were there, tell me in your own words what happened last night. Remember that this is still an unofficial inquiry, so you can help yourself by being as accurate and as truthful as you can."

Leo took a moment. "Earlier, me and J.J. went to an auction at the Luxor that had advertised some of J.J.'s football gear and keepsake stuff. We was impressed. J.J. said it was taken off his place illegally during his arrest and trial for a murder involving his ex-wife Danielle, a couple of years back. He was found innocent of all them charges you know, but his stuff was taken, you dig?"

"So me and J.J. has a few drinks, and goes up to Altman's coop after the auction to politely ask for his goods back. Altman don't want to hear none of that 'give me back my stuff shit,' and gets all huffy and starts prancing around like a monkey see, and tells us to get out. Says if J.J. wants his stuff back, to come to the auction and buy it back."

"Then what happened Leo?"

"Well, this scumbag Altman, who probably got J.J.'s stuff from a fence for twenty cents on the dollar, comes at us to throw us out. The clumsy goof ball, he trips over the coffee table, and goes down and kinda like hits his head on the edge of the table and knocks himself out. He's like unconscious, sleeping like, so me and J.J. just goes into one of the bedrooms, grabs some pillow cases and starts taking J.J.'s stuff." Leo looked up at Detective Gutiérrez trying to get a look of approval from him. It was not forthcoming. "It was all J.J.'s stuff ya know by all rights." Still no reaction from Gutiérrez. "That's all I got to say," and Leo clams up.

"Now Leo, you know that's not entirely true. J.J. bolted out the door so fast, he bowled Officer Giles over, and refused to stop when Officer Lawrence asked him to. He ran down the hall to the stairwell. That sound like a robbery to me."

"Don't know nothin' bout that, I was just helping out, maybe J.J. got nervous, thought those guys in the hall were going to rob him." Gutiérrez gives Leo a quizzical look. "See we both kind of innocent, me, I just be helping J.J. out."

"Well how about this Leo—the pillow case you were filling had a few of J.J.'s collectibles in it, but the rest of the stuff was all baseball related or ice hockey related, like an ice hockey mask."

"Hard to tell the difference in stuff sometimes."

"Sure Leo, you're a former NFL football player am I right?"

"Yeah."

"How many years did you play? Let me guess, four years on some Pop Warner teams, four more years in high school, then four years in college and, nine years with the Oakland Raiders. That's twenty one years of football Leo, and you can't tell the difference between a football and a hockey mask, or a baseball glove from a kicking tee. You were robbing him Leo, plain and simple and you know it."

"He owed us, the son-of-a-bitch, I ain't saying no more."

"And Mr. Altman came at you and took a nasty tumble. A pudgy five foot six, hundred and sixty pound, bald headed little Jewish guy from the Bronx was physically going to throw you two out."

"He came at us," snapped Leo.

"So now he came at you, I thought you said he tripped while he was prancing around." No comment from Leo. "I see you have a nasty bruise on your right hand, Leo. Like on your knuckles, is that new?" Leo looks and says nothing. "The EMTs reported that Mr. Altman's jaw was broken, making C.P.R. impossible."

"I'm done talking to you detective, I want a lawyer right now. Leo knew he had been had.

Upstairs, "He's lying like a rug and hoping J.J. will bankroll him out of this the way J.J. got off the murder charges in L.A.," said Bob.

"So you don't think J.J. was innocent of those murders?" Detective Lawrence, Chief Avery Adams asked sarcastically. They all laughed heartily.

"Okay John," the chief talking to Detective Watkins, "It's your turn. Go see what Mr. Jefferson has to say for himself."

Detective Watkins introduced himself to J.J. with the usual courtesies, then presented him with the charges. Bob had already apprised him of the charges, at the hotel, the night before however, they were enumerated for him again. In his own words he gave a good account of the whole evening including himself and Leo, his bodyguard, at the memorabilia auction. J.J. admitted that they went to the room in the Luxor to ask Mr. Altman if he could have his collectibles back. He said he even made Mr. Altman an offer of ten thousand dollars for the lot of it. He said Mr. Altman was shocked by his offer, and started to look queasy and clutched his chest. He fell down hitting his head on the coffee table.

"You didn't think to help him at that point?"

"No, he looked okay, just unconscious. It was late, we wanted to get going, get home and catch some Z s."

"You were very tired J.J.?"

"It had been a real long day for us officer," as if they had actually been working at something. The police behind the glass window just snickered.

"So why get some pillow cases and start stuffing them with collectibles if you were so tired, J.J.?"

"I just wanted them, sir; I was going to give him a certified check for my stuff, the very next day, I swear it."

"Did he agree to the amount?"

"Seemed like he did to me and Leo."

"Really?"

"Yeah, really."

"Then why didn't you stop and help Mr. Altman, and why did you bolt out the door when Office Lawrence told you to stop?"

"He had a gun, thought he was going to rob me."

"He had a gun, you saw it and ran away."

"Yeah, real fast."

"Faster than a speeding bullet J.J.?" No comment from J.J. "If you saw his gun you would have seen his gold badge as well."

"Didn't see it, happened too fast."

"Okay answer me this, where is the pillow case with the collectibles in it you ran off with?"

"I can't remember, oh yeah, I tripped going out the exit door to the street, and the stuff went flying."

"And you didn't stop to pick it up?"

"I thought there was a crazy man with a gun chasing me, I was running for my life."

"Well J.J., listen to this and rethink what you just told me. When we checked you in here early this morning we took all the things from your pockets and your belt and your shoelaces for safe keeping. It's all standard procedure. We were surprised to find a key to a storage unit out at the airport. We are going to get a court order to open up that box today, you can bet on it."

J.J. looked glum all of a sudden. "I want a lawyer now, this dumb interview is over."

He knew at this point he had been had as well.

CHAPTER ELEVEN

"So our boys lawyered up", Bob said talking to Chief Adams.

"You bet, but we got the goods on 'em now, and J.J., the smart one, he still had the key to a storage box at the airport on him when we arrested him. We got a jiffy court order to open the box, and Bingo, out came all the stuff he had taken from Altman's suite.

On top of that, we interviewed Brad, the panty waist helper Altman had sharing his suite, the one Detective Stiles caught standing there in his pajamas. He heard it all play out, every word J.J. said, and especially what he didn't say. He's pissed about it all and will swear to it in court that J.J. never offered Mr. Altman any ten grand. He said J.J. just demanded his collectible items back and Altman told him no. Brad said he never showed himself as he was in the bedroom in his pajamas. He said he was afraid of J.J. and Leo, because he had seen them earlier in the evening, knew who they were and, was petrified of them."

"A real pussy huh?" added Larry.

"But a valuable one now," said the chief. "He said he heard the punches land; of course he didn't know who threw them, and when his boss sent down and cracked his head, he said he peeked around the corner and saw the two, but was still too afraid to come out."

"What a wimp." Bob added, "Bet he's upset now because now he's effectively out of a great job."

At that moment, in the chief's office Bob, Larry, the chief and detective John Watkins heard a knock on the door. Detective Armando Gutiérrez ushered in a messenger from Las Vegas General Hospital. Dressed all in white from head to toe with EMT badges on both shoulders, and a hospital ID tag on the pocket of his shirt, he introduced himself.

"I'm Peter Saxon, sent here by the doctors attending to Mr. Alan Altman, with news for your ears only. The doctors at the hospital assume that the two suspects you brought in, famous as they are, are lawyered up now, and waiting to be bailed out."

"You are quite correct about that Mr. Saxon, so what have you got to tell us?" The chief asked.

"I'm here to give you some important confidential information that could have significant bearing on how you proceed with the two guys you're holding. It's information you probably don't want the media wonks here in town to hear first. It would get back to the suspects through their lawyers before you even knew about it."

"Okay spit it out, Mr. Saxon" the chief now impatient.

"Mr. Altman died at 8:05 this morning of internal bleeding to his brain caused by a blow to his head, from impact on a sharp solid object. His jaw was broken as well, which hampered the administration of mouth to mouth resuscitation, but it was the blow that killed him, and caused the intracranial bleeding."

"Good God, and all for some crappy sports souvenirs," blurted Detective Gutiérrez.

"So why not just call us to tell us?" asked the chief.

"We don't trust all the ears at the hospital these days. Someone could leak this information to the local media faster than you could blink for a fat finder fee. You would end up hearing it first on Channel 4 at noon. We thought it might hamper your police procedures."

"Right, we had a similar case not long ago and it did mess up our interrogations," said Detective Watkins.

"Good thinking on your hospital's part, to send you, Saxon, we will remember this and where the information came from. Thanks so much for coming over, and please ask the doctors at L.V. General to hold off on an announcement for about 2 more hours while we re-interview the suspects. Say the family has to be notified before the news guys, that's always a good excuse" Saxon left after handshakes all around.

"So, what's the plan now Chief, these guys are lawyered up, and their attorneys are either here with them now, or on the way," said Bob.

"Probably getting ready to spring them out on bail," chipped in Larry.

"Let's re-interview them again right now," stated the chief.

"Get in there with Leontis James right now Armando, tell him new charges are being filed against him, that he killed Altman, and let's see what happens."

Bob and Larry were all ears. They thought their work was done here, but with the turn of events, they thought Altman's death could lead to something much bigger than they had ever anticipated.

"Best we stay and see how this pans out Bob," noted Larry.

"Let's keep a low profile Lar, we don't want to appear to the press or anybody else that we were stalking J.J. and Leo."

"Yeah, and that includes our chief back in L.A."

"Right and it's exactly what we were doing wasn't it?"

"Sorta." They both knew it.

"You'll be out of here in less than an hour," Leo's attorney was saying, starting to stand up as Armando Gutiérrez entered the interviewing room.

"I just had a bail bondsman on the line Detective, as soon as my client Mr. James is arraigned in front of a judge, he's a free man until a trial date is set."

"I've got some interesting news for you two, and I think you'd better sit down to hear what glad tidings I bring." Hesitantly, they did. It'll give you a chance to collect you thoughts" Detective Gutiérrez said smiling. He then apprised them of Mr. Altman's death, and how the hidden witness, the flunky aide, Brad, had heard the whole transaction from behind the bedroom wall. "He said he heard Mr. Altman say no, and then asked you two athletes to leave. Then he heard a punch land, and the coffee table going down, and Mr. Altman bumping his head really hard. He's willing to testify to all of this. He really loved his boss, and is now out of the best job he ever had."

Leo and his attorney went into immediate shock. "To add to your dilemma Leo, I have here in my hand a faxed report from the Oakland Police Department. It shows a whole laundry list of your past misbehaviors complete with a couple of visits to the county prison farm you took as an adult. I'd say it doesn't look good for you Leo, with that nasty bruise on you knuckles, and your history of aggravated assault. You beat up your wife several times, once even in an elevator all caught on video tape. I'd say they are going to fry your sorry ass this time, no plea bargaining or leniency pal."

"Let us have a couple of minutes to conference, Detective; this disclosure sheds new light on the situation."

"I would definitely say so," said Armando as he left the room.

"You handled that great, Armando" the chief remarked. "Now that we've shaken the tree, let's see what falls off."

Back upstairs in the glass paneled listening room, Bob huddled with Larry. This should really be interesting Bob."

"You bet partner, let's see if something pops up out of that safe deposit box now."

Focusing on the activity in the interview room, and just listening to Bob and Larry, the Chief asked: "What's this about a safe deposit box fellas?"

"Nothing, Chief, private joke, let's just see if we can read their lips. Leo and his lawyer were mumbling and whispering to each other, trying to hide their lips with their hands.

Detective Watkins spoke next. "If Leo is going to cut a deal somehow, I'd like to know about if before I get back in the box with J.J."

Earlier, Detective Watkins had been in the interview room with J.J. and his attorney, but he wasn't saying anything of interest, sticking to his original story. His attorney left to make some phone calls, and hadn't returned as yet. He would need to be there with his client for the arraignment with the judge. No doubt he was trying to communicate with the original "Dream Team" in a conference call. This was serious stuff, and not some chicken shit misdemeanor. A two hundred dollar fine and some community service hours would not make this go away. John Watkins was hoping neither J.J. nor his lawyer had gotten wind of Mr. Altman's death yet. He would have the upper hand then with the element of surprise.

Back in Leo's interviewing room, his lawyer signaled for more time pointing to his watch as he looked up to the one way window. Even a rookie lawyer could figure out that Leo would have to take the rap for the murder and spend the rest of his life in prison for his impulsive hit on the auctioneer. The prosecution would have motive, cause, past behavior and a credible ear witness. Leo was a cooked goose, and both he and his attorney knew it. Leo's good buddy J.J. would get off, being an accessory could be beatable, and not seriously affect him. He'd lie and whine under his defense team's directions. He would distance himself from Leo, and the heinous deed saying he entered the suite legally and politely, asked for his collectibles back, offered to pay a reasonable amount. He would say that he offered to negotiate with Mr. Altman, but was refused point blank. Then his Neanderthal buddy with the hot temper, and a history of violent behavior, attacked the poor man and oh…boo hoo, look what happened.

I'm so sorry, I could cry he would say, and thanks to some artfully applied eye drops, he would. The jury would be impressed by his remorse. It would be a case of J.J. saying ten grand, and "ear witness" Brad saying he heard nothing. Brad would have to submit to a hearing test, and then a whole reenactment of the crime scene in Altman's suite would ensue with J.J. talking in very muffled sentences. Of course the only person who really knew the truth was Mr. Altman, and he was gone. Leo could see it all unraveling. J.J. gets a tap on the hand and, Leo gets to spend life with the rump rangers in prison. It was time to play his ace in the hole.

Armando Gutiérrez came back in the room after half an hour and said sarcastically: "You two have enough time to weasel your way out of this one?" He got no reaction out of Leo or his lawyer. His lawyer said he wanted the Chief of Police to come in with two witnesses and a person to record, and verify the statement Mr. Leontis James was about to make. "This is highly irregular," Armando said, "but I'll relay the message." It was not really necessary, the other detectives and the Chief were all listening to, and seeing, what had transpired in the interviewing room.

"Tell them Leo will admit his guilt and make a written statement to that effect as well."

"Wow this is going to be good," John Watkins blurted out.

"Real good," echoed the Chief.

"Can we listen in?" Asked Bob.

"Sure, you two can be part of it in fact, witnesses."

"No they can't, Chief," said Watkins; their presence would muddy the waters; the defense might say his confession was coerced, too many cops."

"Okay, we'll get a janitor and a secretary from the clerical pool to be witnesses."

Back in the interview room, now Leo's attorney opened the proceedings with, "I want these witnesses, and all the detectives involved sworn to secrecy on this confession, and the deal that is proposed if you agree to it."

"Must be a real blockbuster, what with all the stage play and intrigue."

"It is Chief, it really is," said the attorney.

An hour later the story was worked out and accepted by all parties concerned. Leontis with much prompting spilled his guts, and a written confession was made and signed, his attorney helping with the grammar and spelling.

Back upstairs, Bob and Larry were having a celebration, high fiving and back slapping each other. Detective Watkins couldn't understand the magnitude of their joy. "I knew it, I knew it, and the knife is in the safe deposit box."

"Just like Ricky said", stated Larry.

"What's all this about a safe deposit box, and who is this Ricky fellow?" Watkins wanted to know.

"So much for detail John, you have a head to head with J.J. soon, don't you?"

"They haven't called me yet, but knowing what I heard, I'm going to have a hard time keeping a straight face."

"You don't have to let on about the knife that will all be dealt with at a subsequent trial. You can just say Leo cut a deal, and flipped on J.J. He will try to defend himself, and try to blame it all on Leo to save his own sorry ass. His lawyer will tell him to shut up as he, and whoever, try to come up with a new defense plan now. He probably had his own deal all worked out. Wonder if he got wind of Altman dying?"

"It doesn't matter, Leo flipped first." Bob continued, "Any jury in the Western Hemisphere will be biased against J.J. even though none of the murders in L.A. will be admissible or even pertinent in this court trial."

"I'll bet J.J.'s lawyer was tardy getting back here, making plans with the old "Dream Team" or forming a new one. I'm sure he plans to fly his butt out of here as soon as bail is posted."

"Whoops, here comes the desk sergeant fellas," Watkins chirped.

"Watkins, Mr. Jefferson's attorney is here, he wants you in there with them right away."

"Want to watch, guys?"

"Wouldn't miss it for the world," they replied in unison."

CHAPTER TWELVE

J.J.'s attorney, a noted Las Vegas barrister, Erasmus T. Dowd, was more than ready to spring his client, having spent the last few hours making extensive telephone arrangements regarding his situation. He was anticipating imminent release on bail. Bob, Larry, Armando and Chief Adams were looking forward to the fireworks that would go off when detective John Watkins broke the news to the two suspects of Mr. Altman's death. Especially interesting would be the reaction to the new charges leveled at J.J.

Initially they were both stunned, conferenced in whispers immediately, and eventually pulled themselves together. J.J. stuck to his initial story denying all the allegations against him especially the one of him throwing the punch that led to Mr. Altman's demise. Erasmus beat a hasty retreat to make an important phone call. He returned in a half an hour. He whispered something to J.J., and then requested that they see a local judge for arraignment as soon as possible, but not in the company of Leontis James.

Transported in the back of the Chief's Suburban, J.J., Erasmus Dowd, John Watkins and the Chief were taken to the Clark County Courthouse to appear before Judge B.F. Coaster. The Judge was a tall lean man in his mid-sixties, almost bald, yet dapper in smart horn-rimmed glasses, and a colorful striped tie, peeking out of his black robes to perk up his face. A court recorder, radiant in her perfectly tailored business suit, coiffed hair and professionally applied make-up, was teamed with an equally appealing court clerk who read the charges.

Bob, Larry and Armando entered the otherwise empty courthouse room, and sat in the back row near a bailiff guarding the door.

After the formalities of introductions, J.J. and Erasmus stood in front of Judge Coaster, as the court clerk read the charges. "Julius Jefferson you are hereby charged with the second degree murder of Mr. Alan Altman last night at approximately 4am in the Executive Suite West of the Luxor Hotel and Casino, and subsequently fleeing to avoid arrest, and grand theft of sports memorabilia belonging to Mr. Altman. How do you plead, Mr. Jefferson?"

"Not guilty on all charges, your honor."

Now it was Erasmus' turn to speak; "We would like to apply for bail for my client, Judge Coaster."

"In light of your client's attempt to flee last night, and in a well-known case a few years ago in Los Angeles, I'm inclined to deny that request Mr...."

"Dowd, your honor, Erasmus T. Dowd."

"Yes, I recognize your name, Mr. Dowd. You are well known in these parts, infamously, I might add."

Erasmus Dowd was the biggest name in the legal profession in the state of Nevada. He represented actors, prize fighters' musicians, politicians and multi-millionaires who ran afoul of the law while visiting Reno, Las Vegas, and Lake Tahoe. He arranged bail for them, often costing hundreds of thousands of dollars, even millions depending on the seriousness of the charges. Famous personalities were usually not at risk to flee, but occasionally an exception did occur such as that of the notable director of films, Roman Polanski. He is now holed up in a foreign embassy in London to avoid extradition to the United States on rape charges.

"I'm going to set bail at one million dollars for your client Mr. Dowd, and set a court date for a Grand Jury Hearing three weeks hence. Be sure he's here," the Judge, looking up from his calendar, and raising his eyebrows menacingly. "His face is known to many even outside this hemisphere. If he doesn't show up, we will catch him or a bounty hunter will." J.J. cringed when he heard the term 'bounty hunter'. "I'm also impounding his passport until further notice, and restricting his movements to the continental United States. Do you completely understand, counselor?"

"Yes, your honor, we will comply with your directives and I will see that bail is posted immediately."

Chief Adams was pleased. "You guys hand around, Leontis James, and his mouthpiece will be along shortly. See what's up with that and how it goes, and get back to me on it pronto. Watkins, you come with me right now we have work to do." Bob and Larry left the courtroom for coffee and a snack. Armando said he had some phone calls to make and excused himself.

"You know Lar, I think Starbucks is taking over the world even here in this courthouse."

"I know Bob, but I still prefer Seattle's Best, it's a western thing I guess."

"It'll be interesting to see what Leo pleads to now that a deal has been made."

"Interesting yes Bob, and even more interesting to see how our Chief responds to us being here."

As they finished off their coffee and Danish pastry, Bob said, "I guess we're going to find out fast, here comes Leo and his front man."

Leo pleaded guilty to unlawful entry and attempted robbery, and nothing else. His bail was set at ten thousand dollars, and his attorney Jesse Straub posted it for him. A court date was set for him two weeks after J.J.'s, enough time for the media mavens to settle down. Leontis was all smiles, and winked at Bob and Larry on his way back up the aisle to the exit with Straub.

"Shrewd peckerhead isn't he Lar?"

"Yeah, a real scumbag nevertheless, we know he did it and pinned it on J.J. to save his own ass."

"Not much we can do about that now, but I'd like to be there when he pulls that giant pig sticker out of the safe deposit box, and hands it over to the proper authorities in L.A.," Bob was saying when his cell phone rang.

It was his Chief of Police from Los Angeles, Darren Roberts. Bob quickly put his hand over the mouth piece—"it's our Chief Lar, Chief Adams must have called him."

"Listen up Lawrence, I'm faxing a court order up to you and Giles right now. Get it from the administration office there at the Clark County Courthouse, 200 Lewis Avenue, Las Vegas,

Nevada 89101. Fetch it and get on it ASAP. Hot foot it back to that precinct house where Leontis is held, and get him before he's sprung. You have my direct order to apprehend him."

"You mean arrest him?"

"You got it; we have him on a parole violation; he was not supposed to leave California. Transport him back here in your own vehicle, I want him here tomorrow morning, you read me?"

"Understood, Chief. Do we let him pack his clothes and stuff first Chief?"

"Okay, but don't let that turd out of your sight, he's a sneaky little bastard."

"Are you sure this is okay with the Las Vegas Chief?"

"Yup, spoke to him just minutes ago, it's all part of a great big deal we set up for him to trap that shit heal Jefferson."

"Okay, Chief, but do we have to feed him on route?"

"Yes, and keep all your receipts including all yours and Giles, but don't pay Leo James at his hotel. J.J.'s got to put that bill on his own credit card. Oh, and by the way, Leo is going to be put in protective custody until his trial is set, just so you know. Nice work men." Bob could hear laughing on the other end.

"Roberts is thrilled with us Lar, and will pay our expenses for this whole week-end trip. Tell you what, you go back to the Moreno Street Station House, and corral Leo, I'll go check us out of Paris and hook up with you after."

"Be sure to get a receipt Bob, you know what a stickler Roberts is on that stuff, we don't want him to renege on a promise he made over the phone."

"Gotcha Lar, but one thing, aren't you puzzled about this protective custody deal for Leo when we get back home?"

"No, not really Bob, these boys are from the 'hood', you rat out on a brother, especially if he's a key witness in a murder trial, you're born and bred to waste him before he has a chance to talk."

"Whew, just like Godfather and Good Fellows, huh?"

"Right on Bob, and the new "Dream Team", and I'm sure there will be one, they have the clout and the motive to do it. Right now it's Leo's word versus J.J.'s."

"We know who wins that contest, in fact we should watch out own asses until we get back to L.A.".

"I don't think they can act that fast Bob, we'll be on the road in less than an hour, and nobody but us knows about this return deal, not even Dowd."

"And the knife, Lar, if Leo doesn't get the blade out of the safe deposit box to re-open the Danielle Supon Jefferson case, the whole deal would be off."

"Let the big boys figure that one out Bob."

"Okay I'm just concerned, but J.J. doesn't know about the deal Leo made does he?"

"Don't be naïve Bob, he knows, and he's scared shitless. Our chief knows it too that's why we're taking the punk Leo home with us today before the "Dream Team" can line up a hit man."

"But Lar, maybe the "Dream Team" wants to see another big trial in L.A. after the Las Vegas deal is done."

"No Bob, too long, J.J.'s going to do serious time if he's convicted here, and furthermore, who is going to pay for it? They already have all J.J.'s money; he's practically broke, remember?"

"I don't know any way that J.J.'s going to get off if Leo testifies. It's a slam dunk."

"You'd think, but we thought that the first time with his wife and lover boy."

"Well, the least that can happen is we get medals for our part, you know heroism and bravery." Larry thought that was funny Bob had said it facetiously. "Probably another 'Atta boy Award' at the next policeman's ball."

"True, but promotion wise, this is a real plus for the both of us."

"They'll keep us in the shadows as much as possible to avoid any legal complications that's for sure, but you're right about the promotions."

Leo, Bob and Larry headed back to L.A. late that same afternoon. It had taken Jesse Straub a matter of minutes to post Leo's bail. Bob and Larry were on hand later at Moreno Street where Leo was collecting his pocket belongings from a sealed paper satchel. They showed Straub the faxed court order from Chief Roberts in L.A., and Straub was all for Leo leaving. He sensed potential imminent danger if Leo stayed on in Las Vegas. "Guess we don't need to cuff him or worry about him jumping bail," Bob said to Jesse Straub.

"You never know," speaking softly to Bob just out of earshot of Leo. Be really vigilant and don't let him out of your sight, it's my ten grand I posted. Here take my card and call me if anything comes up. I want him to live to stand trial and beyond, this is a big deal for me."

On the highway back to L.A. the three chatted amicably about gambling, football, road conditions, cuisine in Vegas, the engine in the F-250 and anything except the incident at the Luxor. As darkness set in they stopped at a huge casino and hotel just inside the Nevada border, called Buffalo Bills. The barnlike structure was lit up like a Christmas tree, all done in red, white and blue. Buffalo Bills would be the first place on Highway 15 coming across the desert from L.A. for some people wanting to play games of chance and save a couple of hours of driving.

The three men ate dinner, each having juicy rib eye steaks with all the trimmings, but no alcoholic beverages. Bob kept the receipts, and made a quick walk through the main floor with Larry and Leo which was packed with ham and eggers who were hoping the 5% winning margin would be in their favor that night. Back on the road, Larry set the cruise control on 90 mph and the three just sat back to digest their meal and let the F-250 chew up the miles.

Bob opened up the conversation now that they had all friended up. "That was some sweet deal you cut Leo, saved you some heavy duty prison time I'd say."

"What deal? I don't know nothing about no deal."

"Give it up Leo, we were all there behind the glass we know what went down and why."

"Bullshit, you don't know nothing. Mr. Straub, my mouthpiece he said not to talk to nobody until we gets to court. He said he'll prep me real good if I got to take the stand."

Bob, still doing all the talking stayed calm and friendly. "Leo we're not here to queer your deal, in fact we are in favor of it, okay? We know what got you the deal, and where you stashed the knife that killed Danielle and Aton." Leo went silent. A whole minute passed.

"How the hell you know that, you Sherlock Holmes or sumthin? You don't know nothin' about no knife, you tryin' to bait me."

"How about a safe deposit box you opened at the First Union Bank of California on Ventura Boulevard the day after they took J.J. into custody." More silence.

"Jesus Christ you do know about that don't you?" Leo was totally flabbergasted.

"It's because we're good detectives Leo, street smart just like you," piped in Larry.

"You born in the 'hood Detective Giles?"

"Not quite but close."

"So Leo, after the trial in Vegas," Bob speaking again, "we have new evidence to re-open the other trial and get that horseshit alibi that Johnny Hudson came up with tossed out so justice will prevail."

"Is there anything you two dudes don't know?"

"Well yeah Leo, how are you going to get the knife with J.J.'s prints and blood on it out of the box and into evidence to re-open that case?

"You have to do this without incriminating yourself for aiding and abetting a murder suspect," said Larry.

"Don't know—leaving all that shit up to Jesse Straub; all's I gotta do is fetch it and give it to him."

"You know you're going into protective custody don't you Leo?"

"Yeah, for my own protection till all this shit blows over, then I gets a trial, a slap on the hand, maybe six months in a pretty place, not the big house, and then me and Jesse gets to work."

"Work on what Leo, he have a job for you?"

"We gonna write a book together, and maybe a movie to follow. We gonna split the royalties fifty-fifty, and both make out big."

"And you get to skate on the manslaughter sentence too, what a deal."

"Be sure you get it all in writing," added Larry. Leo wasn't listening he was blabbing about cameo appearances in the movie and interviews on daytime television, maybe even with Oprah Winfrey, or The Today Show.

"Well, all of that notwithstanding Leo," offered Bob, "I hope Mr. Straub can figure out where he can send you after all this to get your name changed. There's going to be a lot of really pissed off people out there. They will be looking to do you some serious harm and it's not just J.J. I'm talking about."

"Well, J.J. ain't got no money left and he be in jail."

"I'm talking about Vance Hubbard Leo, he will be exposed too and he's got connections."

"Forgot about that slimy snake," Leo clammed up, sweating now with the thought of a dirty cop with friends in the system hunting him down. This was a worse nightmare than a hit man from J.J.'s "Dream Team".

He perked up in a few minutes. "I be okay detectives, I got me a kicker, could get that scumbag skunk of a cop Hubbard in such deep shit, he never get out."

"Yeah Leo, like what?"

"Can't tell you exactly right now, but I know he got paid, and how much to set up the acquittal of J.J. a couple of years back in the L.A. trial. J.J. told me and also said the money went out of the country to some relative or something. That Johnny Hudson, he's one smart dude."

"We know where the money went Leo, and with your testimony to what you know it could put Hubbard away for life, and save you from being offed."

"I be sure to clue Jesse in on that, save my black ass from that evil prick Hubbard. When the FBI gets all that payoff money back he won't be able to afford cigarettes, much less no hit man." Leo was laughing now everything was all coming together for him. Bob was elated getting more information out of Leo than he bargained for.

Quite pleased he said "Leo, you are really going to love the minimum security facility you are going to for safety. The other inmates are all bankers, investors, realtors and naughty white collar crime types. You could learn how to invest your royalty checks from them."

Larry got with the spirit of the conversation. "You might even learn to swim and play tennis it's like a health spa up there, medical care, dental, and the works."

"Maybe some of them bad boys got a daughter or a niece needs some stud service," said Leo. They all had a good laugh at that comment and then Bob and Leo dozed off while Larry finished up the drive to L.A.

CHAPTER THIRTEEN

Leo was placed in a private cell without any fanfare while Bob and Larry met with the Chief of Police, Darren Roberts. "Good job men, you look fagged out, go home and get some sleep we can discuss this later in my office at 11am. We'll get the blade out of the safe deposit box, and then Leontis James off to the country club before any of the media schmucks even know he's back here in L.A."

"You hope Chief, those pecker heads have antenna like insects for stories like this," Bob stated.

"I know, I know, but we have to get the knife out of the box without them getting wind of it. Let me work it out."

"Here's a card with Jesse Straub's number on it, give him a buzz, he will want to know. Once Leo's up at the 'country club' he will be okay so long as he keeps his mouth shut about why he is really there."

"I'd warn him good on that chief, he thinks he's some kind of celebrity now, and all those white collar guys have cell phones and computers to communicate with everybody, anywhere they want to," said Larry.

"I definitely will, he could really mess things up if he starts even hinting at the deal he's getting and it gets out."

"And he could really fuck himself, and us if a hit man found out where he was and got to him. There's probably a contract on him already if I'm any judge, Chief."

"Okay Larry, you and Bob get out of here, get some sleep, I have work to do." On the way out Bob spoke to Larry in muffled tones so the rest of the precinct, all ears, would not hear them.

"Not even a word from the Chief about us even being in Vegas Lar, notice that?"

"I guess it went without him saying it, we can't even say anything to our families."

"He's all pins and needles about this whole surprise that has dropped into his lap."

"Wouldn't you be Bob? I mean this could blow up in a heartbeat and he'd have plenty of egg on his face."

"See you at 11am buddy, I need a shower and a shave bad."

At 11am the paddy wagon was at the curb at the precinct. Barriers were in place from the exit to the van with patrolmen standing arm to arm behind the wooden saw horses. As Bob and Larry suspected, paparazzi and media photographers were crowded up close to the barriers trying to get a shot, or maybe even a word out of Leonis James all by himself. At 11:15, five officers escorted five prisoners in hooded orange jump suits into the van. With their hoods up, and handcuffed, it was impossible to tell if any of them were Leo James. The van took off to Los Angeles Superior Court at 4848 Civic Center Way for arraignments.

"How the heck did those vultures get wind of Leo's arrival here so darn early in the morning?" Bob wondered.

"Bad news travels fast Bob, and modern technology, the cell phone make it all the easier," stated Chief Roberts. It's these guys business to feed Fox, NBC and the rest of the networks all the crap they can as fast as they can." The press and the freelance photo journalists took off after the van in their own cars hoping to catch another glimpse of Leo at the Civic Center. Back inside the precinct house, the Chief was bellowing orders. "Okay men get Leo's sorry ass out of the cell and into my patrol car. Have him crouch down behind the back seat, and throw a blanket over him. Larry, you and Bob ride in the Suburban, go to Union Bank on Ventura, but pick up Leo's lawyer as this address first," handing them a piece of paper. "It's a Starbucks on the way, meet at the bank in thirty-five minutes, I'll be parked out front in a squad car."

The Suburban with lightly smoked windows, left and two cars followed it. The two detectives noticed that they we being tailed and stopped at a Tim Horton's donut shop, and went in for coffee. Two guys came up and peeked in the windows of the Suburban looking for Leo, but quickly vanished. "Got rid of those two fast, smart enough not to go with the initial diversion, but not smart enough, huh, Bob?"

"Right Lar, what kind of donut do you want?"

Meanwhile, the Chief left the precinct garage with seven other black and white squad cars heading out on shift change for patrol. Chief Roberts, his car fourth I line, had taken off his heavily gold embroidered hat just in case some smart reported was still lurking around. When they rendezvoused at the bank, the Chief, Leo and Jesse Straub went in and down the stairs to the safe deposit vault. They came out minutes later with a telltale oblong object in a brown paper bag. Chief Roberts gave

Jesse Straub a receipt for something, shook hands, and then Roberts and Leo got in the back of the Suburban. The Chief gave Bob and Larry a new set of directions and got out. Another patrol car pulled up and a patrolman riding shotgun got out, and got into the Chief's car, behind the steering wheel. Then the Chief got in and put on his fancy hat.

"Where to Chief?" he asked. "Follow that Suburban, were going to the courthouse in San Fernando, it's at 900 Third Street."

"But chief, the van went to the Civic Center for the arraignment."

"I know Daly, Detective Smithson can handle that assignment the judge in San Fernando knows we're coming for a special arraignment on Leo's parole violation."

The Honorable Mary Gibson had been prepped for the whole experience by the Chief and the now District Attorney, Mr. Earl Lennard and his legal team. She would also be presiding when J.J. returned for his re-trial when Nevada was done with him. The court appearance was strictly a formality, and soon Leo and his two chauffeurs were back on the road to the minimum security prison Leo was going to in Granada Hills Alissa Canyon. The Suburban drove through upscale housing areas, then orchards of oranges, almond trees and an occasional horse farm. As they entered the prison ground through the perimeter guard gate post, Leo remarked," This is sure gonna beat the county work farm." They poked along at ten miles per hour on a gravel road to the reception building.

"You won't have to pull weeds here, Leo," Larry pointed out, "there aren't any weeds."

"And the food's pretty good too, served on real china, no metal trays, you're going to like it here Leo" added Bob.

"And a semi-private room, no bunk beds, but the bathrooms are still down the hall," it was Larry's turn. "Close your eyes and you are back at San Diego State in the athlete's dorm Leo."

"Yeah, but I didn't graduate, bailed out in the draft my junior year." Leo knew he would never graduate even if he stayed there twenty years. He only went to college to play football and try to get into the NFL.

Earlier, back in Las Vegas J.J. was back in the slammer bitching at his lawyer Erasmus T. Dowd about the royal screw job he was getting, and threatening to kill his rat buddy Leontis James for flipping on him. By now, every radio station and television channel as well as every freelance paparazzi were staked out in front of the Court Street Police Headquarters awaiting J.J.'s release. Leo had made a clean getaway, but Erasmus escape plan had taken some time to materialize, and the window of silence had opened up wide. Erasmus had arranged for a limo to pick them up and scoot them away to the private airport for a getaway in a Gulfstream jet, flown in by a member of Dowd's "Dream Team" of cohorts.

Whisked away without a word to the herd of reporters, Erasmus probably muttered "no comment" between the station house and the limo at the curb, at least fifty times. The whole media mob followed the limo, but were thwarted at the entrance to the airport as the chain link gate fence slammed shut in their faces. No matter what magic J.J. new "Dream Team" could conjure up to get him out of the Altman affair, Judge Mary Gibson would be waiting for him. There would be a whole new jury at the San Fernando Courthouse. This lady was a no nonsense judge, and there would be no repetition of the farce, the first trial was...no courtroom television coverage and a totally sequestered jury comprised of San Fernando residents. J.J. had problems.

Back home that night in L.A. Jean, Ricky and Bob sat down to one of Bob's favorite dinners. Jean had made a baked ham with pineapple chunks skewered on to the outside with toothpicks. There were fresh candied sweet potatoes, not canned, creamed spinach and hearts of lettuce salad with Roquefort dressing. "There is apple pie alamode for desert Bob, so leave a little room," Jean said proudly. Bob and Ricky pounced on the sumptuous feast, gobbling it up ravenously, nobody was speaking. Jean picked at her plate, admiring the appetite of her men, and her handiwork. Before they were quite done Ricky opened the conversation.

"So, Leo ratted out his douche bag buddy J.J. huh Dad?"

"Language Ricky," Jean reacted.

"Seems that way son," not missing a bite.

"Just how big was the knife Dad?"

"Don't know Rick, I never saw a knife, what knife are you talking about?"

"C'mon Dad, J.J.'s. J.J.'s up in Vegas charged with murdering some dude over sports memorabilia at the Luxor and you get back in town today with Leo, who is in some kind of secret custody; what gives?" Bob just shrugs and keeps eating. "We know what's going on here, it's all over the television and internet, everything. I'll bet Leo James, the Cro-Magnon wife beater, bad ass, with the hair trigger temper killed that guy, got caught and flipped on his pal J.J. to save his own sorry butt. He had the knife, it was his 'get out of jail free card' and he finally had to use it to save his own skin."

"Jeez Rick that's quite a story, could you pass the sweet potatoes please?"

"Your father's not talking Rickey, he can't, not even to us, its police business, so you keep your opinions to yourself. We don't want any nosy media types poking around here pestering me or your Dad for a story."

"Good point, Jean but Ricky, you made some interesting observations; how's your forensic class going?"

"It's over now, Dad. I'm taking criminal law this semester. I'm seriously thinking about the police academy or the FBI when I finish my degree."

"Well you seem to have a knack for it son," nodding his head approvingly. "You just might." Rick smiled, he had his answer.

At the station house the next day Larry and Bob gave a full report to the Chief of Police and the District Attorney, Earl Lennard of their whole sojourn in Nevada. "None of this must come out in the trial," the D.A. said. "We have to give you an air tight alibi for being there at the right time and using your training, experience and instincts to be instrumental in the arrests that night."

"Understood Sir," together.

"Your stories have to be in complete sync because you will be called to the stand individually and questioned."

The D.A. had been an assistant D.A. during the original Danielle Jefferson, Anton Sartre trial, and was appalled at the outcome. He wanted to see justice served, and would exercise all his power to see it happen.

As an afterthought, Bob related how Leo had said on their ride back from Las Vegas that he, Leo, had a kicker in case the knife would not be enough to clear him of any jail time. Bob filled Lennard in on his trip to Banff Springs, and his certainty that the money Hubbard had been paid was now in a numbered account in the Cayman Islands. "If we are looking for a clean sweep on the Supon-Sartre killings exposing Vance and Hudson, his now deceased attorney, would it be worth a shot?" Bob asked.

"I think we all hate a corrupt cop," replied Lennard.

"Amen to that," added Chief Roberts. "It would just add fuel to the fire of convicting J.J., I don't see how we could ignore it. It all comes together. The thing is we need to get some more information from Leontis James before we can pursue the matter."

"We got him covered on the parole violation Earl, perhaps you can make a deal with the Attorney General up in Nevada to cut Leo some slack on his violations there for his full cooperation here."

"I'm sure I can swing it Chief, our A.G. and their A.G. up in Reno are pals from way back. Not to mention that I have the Governor's ear anytime I want it."

"Leo will be orgasmic if you could make that happen Mr. Lennard, he's got visions of sugar plums dancing in his head now from all the poop Jesse Straub has fed him," Larry Giles chimed.

"I'll bet those folks up in Banff at the Juniper Grove would lie their asses off if they were threatened by their own government for hiding money for a felon in the U.S. They would cough up the Cayman money in a heartbeat I'd bet. If they used the same cock and bull story they gave me when I went up there about winning the lottery in the U.S. and not paying taxes on it they would sing like canaries for sure." Bob told Mr. Lennard.

"Let me come up with a foolproof trap on that one detective, let's take care of J.J. first, and Hubbard second."

"This is all too good to be true," interjected Chief Roberts, a baseball buff. "Remember Tinker to Evans to Chance in baseball history, well now we have Leo to J.J. to Vance, and this will go down in our history books as a triple play."

"Jesse Straub will walk away from all this smelling like a rose with his new meal ticket Leo James, but I doubt it. He's heavy on the slick and light on the substance in my book," the D.A. commented.

"If he doesn't screw himself, he'll screw Leo, that's for sure," Larry added. And Leo's not smart enough to realize he's being screwed by some sharp attorney."

"Let's all break for lunch men, we can work out the details on all this later." The Chief had a healthy appetite, and was no slave to weight control.

Epilogue

J.J. Jefferson's trial was held first in Las Vegas three months after the Grand Jury indicted him. With the expert testimony of Bob Lawrence, Larry Giles and Brad Smith, J.J. was convicted on one count of involuntary manslaughter and sentenced to fifteen years in the Nevada State Prison in Carson City. There was nothing the slick Erasmus T. Dowd or his not so dreamy new "Dream Team" could do to forestall the inevitable. Old Erasmus turned out to be not a very competent trial lawyer. He had plea bargained every other court case in his star studded career. All the other counts against J.J. had been dropped.

Two weeks later, Leo James was tried in Las Vegas for unlawful entry and attempted robbery. Found guilty he was sentenced to six months house arrest and three years' probation. His attorney Jess Straub, Esq. arranged for Leo to serve his house arrest at his secured home estate guest house just outside of Reno. They no doubt would be working together on Leo's book.

The Supon-Sartre trial was re-opened the following fall, with the presentation of shocking new evidence in the case. A blood stained knife had been found taped to the undercarriage of a certain White Mercury Mountaineer that had been towed to Big Al's Scrap Metal and Recycling Yard in East Los Angeles, ready to be crushed for scrap metal. The alert junk yard owner turned the knife in to local police because he suspected skull doggery. The forensic team revealed the finger prints, and blood which matched that of one Julius Jefferson and Nicole Supon Jefferson. This immediately re-opened the now four year old murder case.

Convicted, J.J. was sentenced to life imprisonment without the possibility of parole for the heinous double homicide of his ex-wife Danielle, and her paramour, Anton Sartre. The original "Dream Team" did not make an appearance at the second trial. Once again Erasmus T. Dowd turned out not to be a very skilled trial lawyer.

District Attorney Earl Lennard with the help of Police Chief Darren Roberts, the Union Representative of the L.A. Policeman's Union, and California State's anti-crime czar brought charges against the disgraced but rich retired Detective Vance Hubbard. He was charged with taking funds out of the country to avoid paying taxes. With Johnny Hudson deceased, the initial case against Vance floundered relative to the actual bribe. However, enough pressure was put on the Canadian couple in Juniper Grove though Interpol that they promptly admitted that their cousin Vance was the source of the untaxed funds. They lied through their teeth at first when pressured, just as Larry Giles had predicted. They wanted to avoid prosecution for their part of the tax evasion scheme. The money was then secretly sent overseas to the Caymans. They were completely exonerated for their enthusiastic cooperation on the matter. They claimed total ignorance of the source of the money. Supposedly they did not know how or where Vance had gotten the millions in the first place. Vance received a twenty year sentence for tax evasion, and ironically wound up in the same prison where J.J. was serving his sentence.

Bob Lawrence and Larry Giles were both promoted to the rank of lieutenant when things settled down. Ricky Lawrence was accepted to the police academy right after his graduation from Orange County Community College with an A.S. degree in Criminal Justice. Jean Lawrence got a surprise vacation to the Cayman Islands and Cozumel from Bob on a Carnival Cruise out of New Orleans on her next birthday.

www.ingramcontent.com/pod-product-compliance
Lightning Source LLC
Chambersburg PA
CBHW071403170626
46811CB00003B/1237